# RAMSEY
## A St. Claire Novel

## TINA MARTIN

*Cover image courtesy of Javier Reyes via Unsplash*

Inquiries? Contact:
tinamartinbooks@gmail.com

Visit **Tina Martin Publications** at: www.tinamartin.net.

~ . ~

*He loves her.*

*He shows her.*

*Don't talk about it.*

*Be about it.*

~ . ~

# Ramsey
## A St. Claire Novel

# Chapter 1

Sweet.

That's the one, consistent word that always came to Ramsey's mind whenever he thought of his wife, Gianna. Whenever somebody asked him *how's married life* or on those frequent occasions when his single brothers, Romulus and Regal, swore up and down they'd never become permanently tied down to *one* woman almost like they were trying to convince themselves of it. In all of those instances, Ramsey thought of how sweet life was with Gianna.

He cracked a smile. He loved the permanence of this union with her – embraced it with everything he had – because she was *sweet* in every sense of the word. He knew that better than anyone. He had free reign to make that discovery and what an expedition it was to navigate the plains and curves of her soul. Her body was oh, so sweet.

Sweet to look at.

Sweet to touch.

Sweet to taste.

Even the intangible things he couldn't actually taste like her personality was sweet. She was a kind-hearted person – as sweet as those cupcakes she baked for a living.

She was a little on the timid and quirky side but that's what he found endearing about her. Even after they were married, she was still somewhat shy around him and would often blush whenever she caught him staring at her and he stared often.

He couldn't help it.

He was in love with her – a love that teetered on madness and at times confusion as to how this kind of connection with another human being could be possible. But it was possible – the kind of love that made the hair on his arms raise whenever he gave lengthy thoughts to how they came to be. Love that made him reconsider everything in his life whenever there was a conflict involving her. Love that made him put her first because he wanted to, not because a bestseller or Steve Harvey said that's the way a man was supposed to love his woman. His love for her ran deep into the depths of his body. Deeper than veins, down into the very marrow of his bones.

He was fortunate.

This was the kind of love some people never found, but he knew he discovered it the moment he laid eyes on Gianna at her place of business – The Boardwalk Bakery – and saw a speck of flour on the tip of her nose. He knew it when her translucent, cinnamon-toned eyes connected with his deep, dark ones. Seeking ones. He knew it when he tasted chocolate from her fingers. When he felt her lips quiver against his during their first kiss. The first time he held her nervous, quivering hand. Took her to dinner. Told her he loved her.

Tired of standing in one spot beside the bed and feeling he wasn't close enough to her, he eased down next to her. She was sleeping this time of the night – one in the morning – but he was up – in more ways than one, admiring her. Even while at rest she was radiant, her skin blanketed with a soft glow that made him think of a silk, chocolate soufflé. His mouth watered. She was making him hungry. Her brown hair, still tousled from the love they made just a couple of hours ago, was fanned out over her pillow. Typically a wild sleeper who'd change positions constantly throughout the night, lying on her back was more comfortable these days. Ramsey stared at the reason why – at her growing stomach. This was what all the love they'd made produced – his first child. *Their* first child.

A daughter.

Lately, he found himself wondering how he'd be as a father. How she'd be as a mother. How a baby would change their lives. How he had so much to live and work for. Marriage was as exciting as welcoming his first child and the two came with great responsibilities.

Years ago when he started St. Claire Architects, he had no idea that his passion would grow into a million-dollar organization but it had, and with his brothers as managers and leaders in their various departments, it would grow even more, he knew. When the success came, he was proud that something he started from nothing had sprouted into a great way to make a living. There was nothing more freeing than doing what you love and making a living at the same time. Now, he would not only be taking care of himself, but his family as well. He was no longer working to satisfy his need to be successful or to be mentioned in fancy publications or touted as the top architectural firm in the Carolinas. He was working all for the joy and happiness of *the* sweetest woman in the world and his baby growing inside of her.

Ramsey flicked on her bedside lamp to get a better view of Gianna's resting face and her smooth, brown skin that he couldn't help but touch. He didn't want to touch her for fear he would wake her, but he just couldn't help it when it came to his *cupcake*. He had to – even after they'd made love just a couple of hours ago – he still found an urgent need to touch her. With his fingertips, he traced the curve of her stomach that he found fascinating during her sixth month of pregnancy. He brushed a kiss across her stomach, then placed one on her lips. He watched her lips curve into a beautiful smile.

She stretched and yawned. Her joints crackled as she moaned herself awake. "What are you doing, Ramsey?" she asked, twisting her body toward him so she was lying on her side now.

"Admiring what's mine," he responded in a quick, blunt answer that spoke volumes about the way he was feeling at this precise moment.

"Admiring what's yours," she repeated, eyes batting softly, filled with sleep. Another yawn came and went. "And what might that be?"

"You already know."

She fought fatigue to open her eyes wider and get a good look at her husband. She instantly bit down on her lip. How was it that he looked finer each time she laid eyes on him? His eyes projected threats of seduction. His lips were freshly licked and hungry, waiting for sustenance. His face told the story of desires he'd yet to speak. That all meant one thing – he wanted her again.

She stroked a hand across his beard and watched him close his eyes. "Ramsey, come to bed," she said softly. "You have to work in the morning."

"I'm the boss, baby. I don't *have* to go to work in the morning." He flicked off the lamp then walked around the bed to his side where he slid right up to her and spooned the shape of her so her round bottom was nestled in the cradle of his pelvis while his muscular chest fused with the feminine softness of her back. She smelled good – like the scented berry lotion she'd apply before bed.

"You don't have to, but you will, overachiever," she teased.

He could only smile. She was right, of course. It wouldn't be the first time he went to work after only getting a couple hours of sleep and it wouldn't be the last time, either. "Are you comfortable in this position?" he inquired.

"Yes. I'm fine."

"Okay." He kissed her neck – felt like his lips were gliding across velvet. He felt her body quiver in response. "You and my daughter mean the world to me. Do you know that, Gianna?"

"Yes, Ramsey," she said playing with his long fingers as his hand settled on her stomach. "You tell me that every night."

"And what else do you know about me where you are concerned?"

Gianna smiled. They'd been through this before. "That you love me."

"And?"

"You adore me."

"And?"

Her smiled deepened. "That you'd do anything for me."

"That's my girl," he said, leaving more wet kisses on her neck. He couldn't imagine what his life would be like without her. Years ago when his fiancée died, he never thought his life would rebound like this – never imagined he would be this happy again. But here he was – overjoyed and in love – with a baby on the way.

"What are your plans for tomorrow?" Ramsey asked since the bakery was closed on Mondays.

"I have to place a few orders for food

supplies, then I'll probably swing by Gemma's to see how decorating is coming along for the new place. I'm so glad she and Royal moved to Lake Norman."

"I am, too. I know how close you are with *whittle* sister," he said, teasing her.

She tapped his hand. Came off like a love lick.

"I wanted you two to remain close."

Gianna silently acknowledged his statement, then said, "I'm so proud they found each other. Gemma has been doing so well with Royal. They're perfect together."

"Just like us."

Her cheeks dimpled. "Very much so." She commenced stroking the length of his masculine fingers from the base to his well-manicured, trimmed fingernails. His hands were strong like he was one of the men laboring in construction instead of the guy working behind the scenes. Designing structures. Calling the shots. Closing deals.

"Gianna," he said.

"Yes?"

"Can you turn around and look at me for a minute?" he asked.

"Really, Ramsey? You're going to make me turn this big ol' baby bump around? I weigh a ton, you know."

A smile curved his lips. "You don't weigh a ton. You've barely gained any weight, baby. You're all belly."

"If you say so."

"I know so, now look at me."

"Ugh," she grunted. "You better be glad I love you," she told him, rolling onto her back and then shifted her body in place, getting as comfortable as she could in this new position where the sheets and pillows felt cooler, looking at him now. Dang. It took a lot of energy just to make the turn, but it was well worth it because now, she could see him as clear as day in the semi-darkness of their bedroom. She instantly reached to stroke his beard, one of her favorite features of his face. She loved it – loved the way her fingertips felt across those charcoal black, bristly hairs. Everything about him was off the charts. For one, those deep, pit-black eyes of his could read her so well and it was so easy for her to get lost in them. And then there were those thick brows above those eyes. Lashes that stood out and made his eyes even more magnificent. The straight nose that paired well with his angular, hard jawline.

Lord have mercy...

"Gianna St. Claire?" Ramsey said to get her attention. Once he saw the moment she came out of her trance, he smiled.

Gianna glanced at his teeth then back at his eyes. She smiled back, knowing she'd been caught staring. "How are you so perfect?"

His forehead puckered. "What was that?"

"I asked, how are you so perfect, Ramsey?"

Ramsey's smile deepened as he rested a hand on her waist. He heard her question the first time, but since his sweetheart had the habit of thinking out loud, he figured this was one of those occasions.

It wasn't.

She was *intentionally* asking him this question.

"I'm far from perfect, baby," he said.

"You're not all that far from it. You're—you're everything," she said, then pressed her lips to his. "So, freakin' perfect," she hummed softly against his lips.

"I'm giving you fair warning, Gianna. Stop talking like that."

She giggled. Nibbled on her lip. "Why?"

"You're going to make me want you again."

"That's nothing new. You always want me," she said.

"Yes, I do," he admitted, unafraid of the truth and its freeing effects. He took a kiss of his own, latching onto her lips, taking a deep kiss, savoring her tongue like a delicacy. He delved deeper, using his tongue with skill, twirling it around in her mouth. Then he seized her tongue, pulling it with powerful suction and released it, only to consume her entire mouth in a way that would calm his craving for her, yet the consumption stirred fire-hot coals within him at the same time, causing the blood pumping through his heart to burn with fire, combusting like gasoline.

He wanted her again. Wanted her in the worst way.

"You did this," he said the second he snatched his mouth away from hers and was right back to kissing her again while tugging at the silk fabric of her nightgown for the second time tonight. With an opened hand, he grabbed a handful of her softness while listening to her moan intermittently as they kissed.

He loved it – loved to hear her moan in pleasure knowing he was the reason why she was doing so. Knowing she liked it when he loved her this way.

"Come here," he whispered against her moist lips, lying onto his back.

She already knew what *come here* meant since being pregnant, so she straddled him – one of the few positions that would guarantee the baby's safety. And then she stared down at him – *the* man – her everything as he reached to guide himself to her sweet spot, watching as she closed her eyes and threw her head back as her body took him in. All of him. He absorbed this feeling down to every nerve ending – felt like a new experience every time they made love.

Though their positions had to change, he still required a level of control. He secured her backside in his hands and began controlling her movements, rocking her backward, then forward – carefully – at a steading rhythm he knew she could handle. He rowed the boat while she held on for the ride, trying not to fall over and drown – not yet anyway – while tossing his name in different tones up into the air, those sounds falling down to his lips.

Her hair fell, hiding her face. Calls to him grew louder. More frantic. Desperate. Her hands gripped him at the pecs. She was almost there. He knew by experience. He moved the hair away from her face, saw her, and that was enough to amplify his desire. He squeezed her hips tighter and when he felt her body lock tightly to his and clench him while at the same time hearing controlled screams emit from her throat, he knew it was okay for him to let go, to flood her with his love and release deep moans of his own.

Gianna's body spasmed. Fragmented. Broke apart. All of that, and all at once. Seemed like it would never stop especially when she felt warm nectar uniting them – stuff that made the baby growing inside of her.

Hair fell into her face again and clung to sweat as she panted. Some pants and moans came out loud. Some soft. Whatever the case, she was loved. Thoroughly. He wouldn't have it any other way.

"Are you okay?" Ramsey asked when he could find his own breath.

"Yes," she said between rapid breaths. She eased off of him slowly, returning to her pre-lovemaking position – lying on her side, facing him.

Ramsey placed a kiss on her forehead, and now sweat was on his lips. "I love you, Gianna."

"I love you, Ramsey," she uttered, exhausted and completely spent after having made love twice in the span of four hours. Her eyes were fighting to stay open when she said, "Get some sleep. No more hokey-pokey."

He grinned. "Did you mean hanky-panky?"

"You know what I'm talking about."

He laughed a little. Where she got her

expressions from, he had no idea, but he always got a good laugh off of them. "Okay baby. No more *hokey-pokey*, at least not right now, anyway. I'll *poke* you some other time." He stroked hair from her face with soft touches, watching her fall asleep.

He smiled, completely satisfied in every sense of the word. He was satisfied with life. With everything, and even with the success of his company, he knew that the real happiness he felt was a direct result of meeting and falling in love with this incredible woman one day during a chance meeting at a bakery on the University City Boardwalk – Gianna Jacobsen – who he wasted no time making his wife – Gianna St. Claire.

# Chapter 2

The walk-in closet was its own room, but it provided him with enough space for his exquisite shoe collection, high-end neckties, expertly tailored suits, hats, watches, coats – the whole nine. And everything was neatly arranged down to his suits being organized by color. Today, he wore a navy plaid, Italian Kiton suit with a blue and white striped shirt and solid blue necktie, pairing it with his favorite pair of shiny, black Ferragamo shoes. RSC (Ramsey St. Claire) initial cufflinks with the matching tie clip and one of the silver Rolexes completed his power outfit of the day. He was a firm believer that the way a person dressed had plenty to do with how they felt on the inside, and so every day when he left for work, he looked like a million bucks.

He took his favorite briefcase – the black, leather Givenchy one – and walked into the bedroom where Gianna was still sleeping. She'd probably be out for a while since he kept her up late. He walked up to the bed, set his briefcase on the floor then leaned over to give her a light kiss on the temple, whispering, "I love you, Gianna."

He stayed there staring at her a moment

more, reminiscing about what they'd done last night and how many times they'd done it. That reminded him to leave her prenatal vitamins on the nightstand, along with a bottle of water – something he did every morning. Then he picked up his briefcase and headed downstairs.

"Good morning, Sir," Carson, Ramsey's butler, said when Ramsey walked into the kitchen.

"Good morning, Carson." Ramsey took a sip of coffee that was already on the counter for him. "Ah. Delicious. I'm going to need a lot more of this to make it through the day."

"Late night, Sir?" Carson set a small plate with an egg-white muffin on the counter in front of where Ramsey was standing.

"Something like that," he answered. He took a bite of the muffin and chased it with a shot of coffee. He glanced at his watch. Then he took another bite. Drank more coffee. "What do you have on tap for today, Carson?"

"Maintenance for the St. Claire castle."

Ramsey grinned. His house was huge, but he wouldn't go as far as to call it a castle. "What kind of maintenance?"

"The carpets, for one. They will be steam-cleaned today. I scheduled a routine check for the AC and heating units as well as the backup generator. Oh, and the alarm system is being upgraded today as well."

"Sounds like you have a busy day ahead of you," Ramsey said.

"I'm sure you have a much busier day than I do, Sir."

"You may be right about that. Seems I'm the busiest when I haven't had adequate sleep." Ramsey finished his breakfast and took the liberty of pouring himself more coffee instead of waiting for Carson to do it. "Hey, I need you to keep an eye on Gianna for me today."

"Don't I always, Sir?"

Ramsey saw the concern on his fifty-five-year-old butler's face when he'd asked the question. He looked worried, almost like his job was on the line. Everything Carson did was done in a way that bordered on perfection – from his delicious meals to the way he handled the upkeep of the property – probably the reason Ramsey kept him around for so long. The man knew what he was doing. "You do, Carson, but today, I want to know when she leaves the house, where she goes and when she comes back."

"Is there a problem I should be aware of?"

"No, there's no problem. I just want to know where she is today. That's all. Keep an eye on her for me will you?"

"Not a problem, Sir."

"Good. I'll have my phone on me, but I do have a few meetings today, so text messaging will suffice." Ramsey gulped down the rest of his coffee then grabbed the keys for the Audi. "I'm off to the races."

Carson grinned slightly. "Oh, by the way, Sir, for dinner we'll be having fried chicken per Mrs. St. Claire's request."

Ramsey smiled. "Whatever the lady wants, she gets."

\* \* \*

"Good morning, Mr. St. Claire."

Ramsey glanced over at Judy, his secretary, and offered her a quick smile.

"Good morning, Judy," he replied and kept on toward his office. He didn't ask her how she was, or what she did over the weekend. As far as he was concerned that was none of his business. Besides, he'd never been chatty with her or anyone else in the office besides his brothers. He liked to keep his work environment free of banter and it didn't matter how long he'd worked with his employees. They weren't his friends. They were *employees* and as long as it stayed that way, he didn't have to worry about people getting their roles confused. When you were at work, he expected you to work. If you wanted to do anything other than that, it would have to be done on your own time. He had no qualms about sending people home. Letting people go. Hiring new talent.

"I'll be right in with your coffee," Judy said before he stepped into the office.

"Please, and make sure it's the dark roast. I need an extra kick this morning."

"You got it."

In his office now, Ramsey set his briefcase on the desk and opened it to remove his laptop. He logged in, checked emails and opened the latest draft he'd been perfecting for the Uptown Paris project. After feedback from Basile and his team, he'd made a few adjustments to the front of the building – ones that would make the structure stand out even more so from the bank towers and high-rise apartments nearby. He leaned back in his chair with his fingers tapping on the desk, looking at the drawing but his mind wasn't seeing it. There may as well had been a big picture of Gianna on his screen lying in bed with her belly exposed, bearing his daughter. The further along she got in her pregnancy, the more anxious he became about her. He worried more whenever she wasn't in his sight, hence the reason he requested Carson to keep an extra eye on her, hoping to quell his anxiety. While Gianna didn't have to work today, he still had his reserves about her being at the bakery alone. He needed to hire help as soon as possible.

**To**: Judy Keffer
**From**: Ramsey St. Claire
**Subject**: Ads

Judy,

Please draft up two ads...looking to hire help at The Boardwalk Bakery. Need a baker and cashier. Word the ads however you like. Starting salary for the baker, $20/hr. Cashier $12/hr. Place them in the *Observer* and on Indeed. Let me know if you have any questions.

Thanks,

-

RSC

_____

"Here you are," Judy said as she entered Ramsey's office with a coffee mug that had the company's logo on it and motto: *Where Excellence Meets Infrastructure.* She set it on his desk.

"Thank you."

"You're welcome."

"Before you go, what meetings do I have on the calendar today?"

Judy never knew when her boss would ask, so she made it a point to get to work early every day to go over his entire schedule. That's why she could easily answer, "You have a status meeting at nine, of course."

He nodded. He had a status meeting every Monday at nine with the project managers and whoever else needed to be in attendance, usually his brothers, especially if they had pressing issues that needed immediate attention.

"You also have the meeting with the representative from Glasgow this afternoon."

"What time is that one?" Ramsey asked after just having a sip of coffee.

"It's at 2:00 p.m."

"Good. Thank you."

"You're welcome, Sir."

"Hey, I sent you an email a few moments ago regarding some ads I need to be placed. If you can get to those before the end of the day, I would greatly appreciate it."

"Will do."

Ramsey looked at the drawing again. He sipped coffee while tweaking the design for the umpteenth time. As an architect, revisions are what took up most of his time, and since he wanted his designs near perfect, he didn't mind the revision process. He welcomed it.

Again his mind drifted to the time Gianna watched him work at his home office. He even let her try a hand at a few lines and angles something he'd never allowed anyone else to do. Only Gianna.

"Excuse me, Sir," Judy said after she tapped on the door and peeped into his office, taking him out of his reverie.

"Yes, Judy?"

"The team is waiting for you in the conference room."

His forehead knotted. "Why there? Status meetings are usually held in my office."

"Well, Sir, if you recall, you were going to meet with CitySites Landscaping this morning but they had to reschedule and—"

"And you didn't move the status meeting back into my office."

"No, I did not. My apologies, Sir," Judy said, sounding nervous. "If you would like I'll have the team meet you in here."

"No. There's no need to reshuffle everyone else when I'm the only person missing," Ramsey said standing up, folding his laptop closed.

"Again, my apologies, Sir."

"Don't worry about it, Judy," he told her.

Judy had proven to be a superb secretary over the years. A few hiccups here and there wouldn't taint her excellent service to him and his organization.

Taking his coffee along with his laptop, he walked toward the conference room. He could hear the men talking as he approached, but he wasn't aware all of his brothers were going to be in attendance. They're sat Royal – the company's troubleshooter, Romulus – the person responsible for securing land for building projects and then Regal – an architect just like Ramsey. The other two men, Ralph Sheppard and Gilbert Lewis were project managers.

"Good morning, gentlemen," Ramsey said in his morning, let's-get-down-to-business baritone.

"What's up, bro?" Royal asked, foregoing formalities just for the heck of it. He, as well as his brothers, knew how formal Ramsey was at work. It wouldn't kill him to loosen up a bit – at least from *their* perspective – but at work, he was all business.

"Good morning," Romulus and Regal said followed by Gilbert and Ralph.

Ramsey took a seat, opened his laptop again then looked at the Paris drawing. Getting right to it, he asked, "Regal, what's the latest on Paris?"

"Everything is all about Paris these days," Regal commented. "Let's see—Basile was impressed with the preliminary building design. You're working on the tweaks now which I assume will be ready when Basile is here next Monday to see the construction site."

"Yes, it'll be ready," Ramsey said. *That's if I can stop daydreaming about my wife...*

"Romulus, you were aware of Basile's visit I hope."

Romulus glanced up from his notes, looked at Ramsey and responded, "Yes. In fact, I would like for everyone in this room to join me for the site tour. I think Basile will be more confident about the project when he sees the collaboration of the team. This really was a team effort."

"I like that approach, too," Ramsey said, "So, block out some time on your calendars and plan to be at the site on Monday. Romulus, email everyone with the details and find a nice restaurant close by where we can sit down and have lunch afterward."

"Yep. It's already a part of the plan," Romulus said, tapping his yellow legal pad with a pen. "I'll make lunch reservations at Palm."

"Perfect." Ramsey glanced at his phone to see if there were any messages from Carson. There wasn't which meant Gianna wasn't up just yet. Or maybe she was up – just hadn't made it downstairs yet. He wondered...

"Do we still have that meeting with Glasgow today?" Royal asked.

Ramsey tucked his phone in the upper left breast pocket of his suit jacket. "Yes. They're sending one of their sales managers directly from Paris. An American guy. I'm sure he's already in town. Let's make sure the meeting begins promptly."

"In your office correct?" Royal asked.

"Yes. My office." Ramsey felt his phone vibrate against his chest. "Ralph, Gilbert—do either of you have any issues to discuss?"

"Yes," Ralph said. "Can you make some time to check out the landscaping at the University City site, Sir?"

"Who did we use for that, Ralph?" Romulus asked.

"It was CitySites, wasn't it?" Regal asked.

"Yes, and I think they did a good job," Ralph said.

"Why wouldn't they?" Royal asked. "We've been using CitySites for all of our landscaping projects."

"Correct," Ralph said, "But if you recall from our previous status meetings, I thought their work was becoming too repetitive. Every site is basically the same, so I had them switch it up from the norm for University City...wanted Ramsey to check it out to see if he liked the new style and to see if there are any design elements we can use for the Paris site."

"Good idea," Romulus said.

"That's *if* we're planning on using CitySites for the Paris building. Are we, Ramsey?" Regal asked.

All eyes went to Ramsey who'd been staring at his phone. He heard the conversation between the men but he was more interested in the text message he received from Carson:

**Carson**: Mrs. St. Claire is up...said she didn't want

breakfast, Sir. I talked her into eating a small bowl of oatmeal and blueberries.

**Ramsey**: Good. Thank you, Carson.

**Carson**: Welcome. FYI, she's going to her sister's place right after breakfast.

**Ramsey**: She's already dressed and ready?

**Carson**: She is, Sir.

**Ramsey**: Okay, thanks.

The conference room was quiet except for the *tick-tock* of the oversized clock above the projector screen.

"Ahem," Regal said, hoping to garner his brother's attention.

Ramsey put his phone away and said, "Yes, we are using CitySites for the Paris building. Ralph, let's plan to meet at the UC site Thursday morning at ten. Will that work for you?"

"That'll be fine with me."

"Good. I'll have Judy put it on the calendar. Anything else?"

"Not for me," Regal said.

When Ramsey didn't see any indication that the others had issues to discuss, he said, "All right. Meeting adjourned. Thanks, fellas."

Ramsey got up, took his laptop and was the first to leave the conference room.

Royal caught up with him before he could reach his office and asked, "Hey, you good?"

"Yes, I'm good. Why wouldn't I be?"

"You seemed a little distracted back there, and I'm sure it wasn't my imagination."

"I'm good," Ramsey said again. When he

came up to Judy's desk, he said, "Judy put a meeting on the calendar for Thursday from ten to eleven with Ralph Sheppard. Meeting location is the University City site."

"Okay," Judy said, scribbling notes.

"And block out my calendar from eleven to five after that. I'll be off that afternoon."

"Will do, Sir."

"Thanks, Judy," he told her and continued on to his office with Royal trailing behind him.

"How are you doing, Ram?" Royal asked, taking it upon himself to close the door behind himself as he entered Ramsey's office.

"I'm great. What about you? Any pertinent issues we need to discuss?" Ramsey asked.

"Ram, come on man. I know you're all work and no play at the office, but it won't kill you to loosen up a little."

"You know how I feel about discussing our personal lives at work."

"But it's not that much of a distraction. Besides it's just me sitting in your office right now so you don't have to worry about the other employees actually finding out you're a real human. Your secret is safe with me."

Ramsey glanced across his massive desk at his brother. These days, he felt closer to his brother, Royal, when before the two always butted heads, especially when it came to work but since Royal married Gemma, they had something in common. They were the only St. Claire brothers who were married and making it extra special was the fact that they married sisters – Ramsey to Gianna and Royal to

Gemma.

"Okay. I'll bite," Ramsey said. "How are you treating my peanut?"

A smile came to Royal's face. *Peanut* was Ramsey's nickname for Gemma. "Good. She's..." Words escaped him as he searched for the most magnificent ways to describe her. "Can I just say that I never thought I could be as happy as I am right now?"

Ramsey smirked. "You got it bad, huh?"

"I do. I'm not even going to lie about it. I am head over heels in love with Gemma."

"That's good. She's good for you. It still baffles me how hard you fell for her. When I told you to watch after her when she was at the hospital, I didn't know you would end up asking for her hand in marriage."

Royal thought back to when he met Gemma. She was sick but beneath what cancer had threatened to do to her, she fought with all her might and chose life. And she was full of life – ready to live. So was he. "Yeah. You made a love connection and wasn't aware of it. She's my heart."

"That's a wonderful feeling isn't it?" Ramsey asked. It's the same way he felt about Gianna.

"It is...makes life so much more enjoyable." Royal stretched and wished he hadn't left his coffee on his desk. "How's life when you're expecting a little one?"

Ramsey couldn't mask the smile that came to his face if he wanted to. "It's nothing short of bliss. I can't tell you how many times I've imagined holding my baby girl and loving her as much as I love her mother."

Royal nodded.

Ramsey sipped coffee, glancing at Gianna's picture on his desk. "I'm going to tell you something, Royal. Life has a way of making you realize that the things you *think* you don't want are the very things you need."

"That's true," Royal agreed. "After all, I didn't set out to get married, but now I get it. I used to frown at people when I asked them how they knew they'd found the one and they would answer that they just knew."

"Yeah. I recall you throwing a few of those frowns my way."

"I did," Royal said. "But, I get it now. Gemma's amazing. There's no way I wasn't going to go ahead and lock her down." Royal leaned back in his chair, stretched, still thinking about coffee.

Ramsey glanced up from his computer to ask, "So, Gemma took a day off to do some housework, huh? Or did she just take off because she knows Gianna's off?" Ramsey looked at his email inbox, accepting Judy's meeting invite – the one he just told her to make for Thursday.

"What you talkin'? Gemma's not off today. We left the house this morning at the same time, actually."

"Really?" Ramsey frowned but quickly cleared his face of the confusion. Carson told him Gianna was going to Gemma's after breakfast. Last night, Gianna told him the same, but how could she be helping Gemma when Gemma was at work?

"Yeah, she went to work," Royal said. "Why? Are you stressing? Think she's doing too much?"

"No. I know she's okay," Ramsey said taking out his cell phone again. He saw a text from Carson five minutes ago.

**Carson**: She just left.

He glanced at his Rolex: **10:42 a.m.** Then he replied:

**Ramsey**: Where did she tell you she was going?
**Carson**: To Gemma's, Sir.

"Let me get out of your hair. You look like you're knee-deep in something," Royal said, standing. "Thanks for the chat. See—it's good to be *normal* sometimes at work, ain't it?"

Ramsey narrowed his eyes as Royal exited the office. Where was Gianna going? To the hospital to meet Gemma maybe? Or did she have to go to the bakery? He was seconds away from calling her when he put the phone down and decided to focus on work. He trusted Gianna, so it really didn't matter where she was going. He was sure they'd discuss it over buttermilk, fried chicken tonight.

# Chapter 3

She couldn't tell if it was morning sickness, an upset stomach from the blueberry oatmeal Carson convinced her to eat, or if her unsettled stomach was due to the fact that she agreed to meet with her mother at Jetton Park this morning. That feeling only intensified when she realized Geraldine was already there sitting on a green, wrought iron park bench along one of the walking trail.

Walking along the sidewalk while runners breezed by huffing and puffing, keeping up their strides, Gianna approached the bench where Geraldine was sitting and said, "Hi, Geraldine." She would never be comfortable enough to call her *mother* even if they did somehow manage to get back on good terms. She'd never been a mother so Gianna didn't feel she deserved the honor of that title.

Geraldine stood up and wrapped her arms around her daughter. Gianna's first instinct was to push her away since she considered such an action to be fake coming from Geraldine Crawford, but she reluctantly accepted her embrace. She had high hopes for this meetup – that for the sake of her child, she could take the steps needed to build a good relationship with her mother, but she couldn't do that without Geraldine's cooperation.

Ramsey didn't care if she let Geraldine go entirely. He said she didn't need the stress that consumed her whenever Geraldine was the topic of discussion and for all intents and purposes, he was right. Gianna knew it, hence her decision to keep this meeting a secret from him.

"Hi, Gianna. It's good to see you." She reached to touch Gianna's stomach, but Gianna blocked her hand.

"Oh. Sorry. It's just a habit to want to touch a pregnant woman's stomach I guess."

"I'm finding that to be true and annoying. I'm very protective of my baby and so is her father."

Geraldine nodded. "I'll keep my hands to myself."

Gianna sat down. Geraldine's strong perfume made her nauseous and lightheaded. Did she really need the whole bottle? And why was she dressed in ripped jeans like she was a college student who'd taken a wrong path in life? She wore a white blouse, her signature gold rings and a pair of camel-colored wedges.

"You're going to be a good mother, Gigi—I meant—Gianna. That, I can already tell."

More runners passed. A skinny white lady jogging while pushing her baby in a stroller. A group of teenagers who looked like they were running just to fulfill a P.E. assignment. Older people – like senior citizen old – who hobbled along the trail like they were waiting for the

Aleve to kick in.

"I wasn't a good mother to you or Gemma. I know that. It's hard to admit, but I know I didn't do right by you girls."

"Why not?" Gianna asked since Geraldine was open to conversation. "Why weren't you a good mother? Whether or not to be a good mother is a choice like anything else in life."

"They may sound crazy to you, but I do have my reasons."

"Which are?"

Geraldine sighed. "I watched my mother—your grandmother—work her fingers to the bone. And I mean this woman worked hard to only bring home pennies. After watching her struggle, I decided I wasn't going to live that way. I'm embarrassed about it now, but my way out of poverty was to find a man with money. And I found your father."

"Jerry," Gianna said, putting the pieces together. She glanced over at Geraldine and noticed that her hands were shaking.

"Yes. He wasn't homeless when I met him. He was a businessman—had a nice home, nice cars, he dressed nice—he had it all. We were planning on getting married and then he lost his job and my plans fell by the wayside. I couldn't marry no man that didn't have a job. I didn't want to struggle. I was already pregnant with you. He didn't know it at the time, but I was. How was I supposed to have a baby with a broke man?" Geraldine crossed her legs. Took a breath. "I panicked—went into survival mode and went on the search for another man that had money. Wasn't hard to do. Men think with the brain they have downstairs. The other one is useless. So, they see a good-looking, light-skinned woman come prancing along—your mama could get any man she wanted. But eventually, seemed the money always ran out, so I found myself bouncing from man to man until I met the man who could give me the financial freedom and stability I deserved. His name was—"

"Let me stop you right there," Gianna said, thoroughly disgusted. "I don't care what his name was. I didn't come here to get lessons on how to be a hoe."

For a moment, Geraldine wanted to snap – to remind *Gigi* of who it was she was talking to and demand respect – all that crap she used to do in the past. Instead, she maintained her composure and said, "Right," sounding defeated.

"What's going on in your brain that you think the only way to find happiness in life is to find a man with money to shack up with and live off of? Why couldn't you have gone to college and figured out a way to make a life for yourself?"

"College..." She shook her head. "You gotta have money to go to college and my mother was poor. You can't save money for college when you have to eat and keep the lights on."

"Even still, Geraldine, there're grants, loans—you could have entered the workforce even without a college degree. What shame is there in starting at the bottom and working your way up?"

"Doing what?" Geraldine said, heated. "I had no skills. I was flirting with the idea of stripping before I met your dad."

*Stripping?* Gianna's eyes flashed disappointment. Felt like she was talking to a child. "Everybody has a skill or *something* they're good at, Geraldine, and I'm sure shaking your butt while men throw one-dollar bills doesn't classify as a talent."

Geraldine uncrossed her legs and recrossed them the opposite way. With nostrils flared, she asked, "You think just because you know how to bake them silly cupcakes that everyone has a talent?"

Ignoring the 'silly' comment, Gianna said, "Yes. I do believe we all have something we're good at—something we can do to make money without relying on someone else to hand you a paycheck. My husband is good at designing buildings."

Geraldine didn't add to the subject of Gianna's husband. She knew Ramsey didn't like her. There was no need to stir the coals to that fire.

"Look, I think we're getting off topic," Gianna said. "The truth is, no child should have to suffer the way me and Gemma suffered."

"You're right. You are absolutely right and I apologized to you for that right as we began this discussion, Gianna. So, why can't you let it go?" Geraldine threaded her hands together. Gold rings overlapping gold rings on old-looking fingers. "All this happened years ago.

You're grown. Married. Gemma's grown and married. At some point, you have to let it go."

"It's so easy for the *offender* to ask somebody to let something go." Gianna frowned. Tears easily came to her eyes. "This has affected me my entire life, Geraldine. You don't understand how all I wanted was to be normal, but I couldn't be normal. I had to be a provider and a caregiver. I had to take care of Gem. I never understood how, as a mother, you could detach from your kids and put a man or your *dreams* of living a wealthy, fabulous life ahead of your children. Honestly, the wealth, the money—it doesn't matter when it's all said and done. Relationships matter. Your *children* matter. I couldn't begin to comprehend the thought of abandoning my daughter like you abandoned me and Gemma." Gianna sniffled, pinching tears from her eyes.

"I don't know what else to say," Geraldine admitted. "I'm sorry."

"Are you?"

Geraldine's leg bounced up and down. Hands were still shaking. "If I could take it back—have a lil' do-over, maybe things will be different."

Gianna wasn't buying that line. It was easy for someone to say what they would do in hindsight simply because they didn't have a chance to prove it. It was all words. All *coulda, shoulda, wouldas*. If Geraldine wanted to make their situation better, she needed to lay out how she would repair their non-existent relationship going forward – not talk about what she should have done back in the day.

"Unfortunately, you can't go back and fix anything. None of us can. You have to focus on what you can do right now and going forward to fix this."

Geraldine's hands fidgeted as she said, "I've developed an alcohol problem over the years. Half the time, I'm not myself."

*More excuses.* Gianna heaved a sigh and placed her hand on her stomach. Her growing baby kept her calm. "Have you tried to get help?"

"No, but it's on the agenda. I'm not sure where to begin."

"Do you *want* help?"

Geraldine stood up. Stretched. Walking back and forth in front of Gianna, she explained, "I do. I don't want to be this person anymore, Gianna. I want my family back."

"Then if that's true, you have a lot of repairing to do, but guess what? That all starts with you."

"I know...gotta start somewhere, right?" She turned her back to Gianna and stared out into the greenery. The peaceful surroundings. The birds chirped. Children played. People were still jogging. "I want to be there for my grandchild. I want to be a mother to you and Gemma."

Gianna wasn't sure how to take this or what to make of it. She wanted to believe her but history showed she'd be let down once again. "Maybe you should reach out to an AA support group."

"Yes. I'll do that," Geraldine said. "I also thought about some counseling."

"It wouldn't hurt. In the meantime, just know it's going to take a long time to repair the damage you've done so don't expect us to welcome you back into our lives so easily."

"I understand. All I want to know is that I have a chance to get back."

"There is a chance, but it's all riding on what you do from this point forward."

"Understood."

Gianna glanced up at her. She still couldn't believe this woman was the same woman who was acting a pure fool in the hospital when Gemma was sick. Now, she was practically begging for a second chance.

* * *

Gianna browsed the shops on the strip, waiting for Gemma to arrive back in Lake Norman. They were going to meet for lunch then go back to Gemma's place to do some decorating and organizing. Gianna stepped out of a gift shop called Heart & Soul where she'd purchased a birthstone necklace for herself and Gemma when she saw Gemma pull up in her Jeep Compass and parallel park on the street like a pro. She hadn't been driving long, but from the looks of things, she learned pretty fast.

She waited for her to get out then wrapped her in a smothering embrace. "Look at you all grown up," Gianna said, "And kudos for not hitting that light pole."

Gianna giggled. "You're never going to let me live that down, are you?" Gemma said, referring to the time she backed Royal's Tesla into a light pole.

"I'm only kidding. You're driving really well—can definitely parallel park better than me. I'd still be sitting there with my blinkers on trying to determine if my car would fit."

Gemma laughed.

"I'm so serious. I even bumped somebody's car once and took off."

"Oooh...aren't you dangerous," Gemma quipped.

"Whatevs. Hey, I bought you something." Gianna took out the birthstone necklace and handed it to her.

"Thank you," Gemma said, admiring the piece. She immediately put it on, then the women headed to the restaurant.

"So, guess who I met up with today."

"Who? Ramsey? And then y'all locked the office door and went at it." Gemma laughed.

"No. Get your mind out of the gutter. I met with Geraldine today." Gianna opened the door to the restaurant, allowing Gemma to enter first.

Gemma gasped and placed a hand over her heart. "You didn't..."

"I did, and I have to say I was shocked by her demeanor."

They sat at the table where they had a good view of the street. Upon being asked by a waitress, they both settled for salad and for their drinks, fresh lemonade.

"I can't believe you met with Geraldine Crawford," Gemma said. "Was she wearing all white again?"

"What's wrong with her wearing white? I suppose that's better than her in all black."

"No kidding."

Gianna grinned. "But no, she wasn't wearing white. She actually looked normal in a *jeans and blouse* kinda way. I was surprised."

"What about the rings? Was she blinged out again?"

Gianna smirked. "Yeah, she still had the rings, girl."

"The last time I talked to her, she told me I needed to wear a wig. My hair wasn't as long as it is now," Gemma said, playing in her curls, deciding she liked it much better when Royal did it. "And then she was attempting to speak Spanish—telling the waiter she wanted a *mucho margarito*—not margarita—margarito."

Gianna laughed. "I shouldn't be laughing. She told me today that she has a drinking problem."

"Really, because you can't blame everything on alcohol."

Hands up, Gianna said, "Hey, don't shoot the messenger. I'm just telling you what she said. I'm not sure if I believe her just yet. Some people are naturally crazy. They don't need alcohol or anything else."

"So true."

Gianna sipped lemonade right after the waitress set the glass in front of her. "Mmm...so good."

"It is," Gemma said after tasting hers, "Although I better not drink it all. Royal would have a stroke."

Gianna smiled. "Hey, did Geraldine ever tell you who your father was?"

"She did. A man named Logan Spriggs, and before you ask, no, I didn't look for him. I don't want to, at least not yet, anyway."

Gianna nodded understanding completely. "Anyway, I don't know if he's serious, but Geraldine says she's going to get help...says she wants to be a part of our lives."

"Eh...I'll believe it when I see it," Gemma said.

"My thoughts exactly." Gianna rubbed her stomach.

"How's everything with the baby?"

"She's growing little by little every day. Ramsey is in love with her already."

"Well, that's not surprising considering how madly in love he's in with you."

A smile lit up Gianna's face. "Yeah, just like Royal is *madly* in love with you."

Gemma smiled. Blushed. "He is, isn't he?"

"Yep."

When the salad arrived, Gemma started on hers right away, then looked up at Gianna. "Hey, let me ask you something, and I hope it's not too personal but when you and Ramsey make love, is he like—um...dominant? Aggressive? Take charge?"

Gianna raised a brow. "You hope *that's* not too personal—talking about our sex lives?"

"Okay, I see what you mean but I just want to know."

"Why?" Gianna questioned.

"Because when—" Gemma paused, glanced around to make sure no one was in earshot of her then continued in a careful, low tone, "When Royal makes love to me, Gianna I swear it feels like an out-of-body experience. I feel like my body isn't mine—like he has ownership of my soul. Like I've died and he gives me life with his love. Jeez, I'm getting hot just thinking about it."

"That's why you're turning red?" Gianna laughed.

Gemma was chuckling, too, while she fanned herself.

"That must be a St. Claire thing because I feel the same way when I'm with Ramsey. It's so intense—like just when I think I've had enough, he triggers something inside of me that stimulates me for more. And Ramsey—goodness—he's so thorough. A straight-up perfectionist. He's so attentive to every move my body makes. I swear he can read my mind."

"Yep...they're definitely brothers," Gemma said smiling.

"Overall, how do you like being married?" Gianna asked.

"It's new," Gemma mumbled with a mouth full of salad. "I like it because I love Royal so much. It's still an adjustment, though. I never thought I'd get married, especially so young. And it takes a huge amount of trust to let a man lead you in the right direction, you know. Do you get what I'm saying?"

Gianna nodded as she ate her salad.

"How did we end up with such strong, amazing men?" Gemma asked.

"You ask the question like that's a bad thing."

"No, not bad. I'm asking because I still can't believe it. I'm married, you're married and I feel like we could have ended up with anyone but we have these intelligent, confident, successful strong men."

"That reminds me of something Geraldine said today...said she was with my father because he had money and he was going to be her way out of poverty. Then when he lost his job, she left him and moved on to the next man and so on and so forth. It got me thinking that even if Ramsey wasn't a brilliant architect—I don't care if he was a mailman or a pizza delivery guy—I'd love him just the same. His money was never a gauge as to whether I'd give him the time of day, but in the back of my mind, I think Geraldine looks at it that way—like we got it made because we married these strong men. Wealthy men."

"Yeah, well who cares what she thinks. We've had to be *strong* all of our lives, thanks to her, with no one to lean on but each other. I did more *leaning* on you than you on me," Gemma admitted, "So maybe these men *are* our knights in shining armor, coming to our rescue."

"Just when I thought you'd given up the Hallmark channel..." Gianna took a sip of lemonade.

"Hey, have you chosen a name for the baby yet?"

"No. Ramsey thinks we should ask the family for name suggestions at the baby shower."

"That's a good idea. Any word from Bernadette on when it's going to be?"

"She said she would let me know at this month's Sunday dinner."

"Cool."

"Are you and Royal going to make it?"

"Of course. I love our family dinners. I love being a part of a family, period. When I would watch these family-oriented movies, I used to dream of a time when I would sit at a large table and share dinner with a family. I love it."

"Me, too." Gianna finished her lemonade. "So, what needs to be done at your place?"

"Not much. Royal decided to hire an interior decorator so I wasn't stressed out about anything."

"Nice."

"I do, however, need to come up with a color for the family room and pick out a sectional sofa. Maybe you can help me with that."

Gianna beamed with joy. "Sure, I can help with that. This is going to be so much fun helping my *whittle* sister decorate her house."

"Oh gosh, Gianna. Give it a rest with the *whittle* stuff."

"Nope. You know you love it."

Gemma narrowed her eyes. "You really believe that, don't you?"

"Sure do." Gianna took out her wallet and slid cash in the check billfold to cover lunch and the tip. "Let's get out of here. I need to be home in time for dinner."

"We practically live in the same neighborhood. You have plenty of time to get home for dinner."

"Yes, but I'm making Ramsey's favorite cupcakes for dessert tonight."

"Oh, that's what it is. Gotcha. All right. Let's go."

# Chapter 4

Judy's knuckles pattered on Ramsey's office door before she opened it and said, "Sir, Mr. Copeland is here from Glasgow Industries."

"See him in please," Ramsey told her. He was already prepared and ready for Mr. Copeland to arrive. Royal was there reviewing the portfolio with him again and he still had Glasgow Industries' website up on his laptop.

When Judy opened the door to invite Mr. Copeland inside, Ramsey walked up to the man, gave him a firm handshake and looked him in the eye – something he did to help him get a feel for his comfortability level in working with a new supplier. A company was only as good as the people running it – didn't matter how good the products were. If he got a bad read from Mr. Copeland, he'd keep it moving. Fortunately, he got a good vibe from the man and he gave a single nod of approval to Royal, letting him know that the guy was okay to deal with.

"Mr. Copeland, this is my brother Royal St. Claire who happens to be the troubleshooter for this fine organization."

"Nice to meet you in person, Royal. I believe we spoke briefly over the phone."

"We did, and it's nice to meet you as well," Royal said shaking the man's hand.

"Have a seat," Ramsey told the guy. "Can I get you some water or anything else to drink?"

"Water will be good right about now."

Ramsey walked over to the wet bar and filled a glass with ice. Then he took a bottle of Voss from the fridge and walked it over to the conference table.

"Thank you," Mr. Copeland said.

"You're welcome." Ramsey sat down. "So, getting right to it, St. Claire Architects has a contract for a new construction in Uptown. Royal visited Paris to study the architecture as well as find a supplier who could meet our needs for specific building materials. Having a supplier in the states will be a huge convenience for this project."

"Yes. As I'm sure you're aware, we have a local branch located in Norfolk, Virginia."

"I can't tell you how relieved I was when I saw that," Ramsey said. "Initially, I thought we'd have to procure everything overseas."

"Not at all, Mr. St. Claire. Now, granted there may be some design elements we may not carry in our Norfolk facility. Those will have to be ordered directly from our main facility in France."

"Understandable," Royal said. "That would also mean that we are proactive about which design elements we may have to order in advance so there's no lag in construction."

"I agree," Ramsey said.

"Such being the case, how would we handle

storage of these special order items?" Royal asked. "I suppose we could leave them at the site if push came to shove."

"We can hold these items at our warehouse and ship them to you as needed."

"Beautiful," Royal said.

Ramsey chuckled. "*Beautiful*, indeed."

"Look, we've done our research on St. Claire Architects," Mr. Copeland said. "I've seen the article in *Architectural Digest* that featured St. Claire Architects. You and your brothers are trailblazers in the design-to-construction business. It's good to see a firm that has the all-in-one package and you do it flawlessly."

"Thank you," Ramsey said. "It's all hard work, no play."

Mr. Copeland chuckled. "I bet."

Ramsey glanced at his phone.

**Carson**: I called Gianna to check up on her. She confirmed she's at her sister's
**Ramsey**: Are you sure?
**Carson**: Yes, Sir.

*Didn't Royal tell me Gemma was at work today?* Ramsey's brows knitted as he glanced up seeing Royal and Mr. Copeland looking at him. How was Gianna at Gemma's if Gemma was at work?

"Mr. Copeland, if you have time, I would like to go over the preliminary requirements for the project. That way, I can get an idea of the products you already have versus the kind of items we'd have to order."

"Of course," he responded.

Ramsey stood up. "Just give me a few minutes. Royal, let me speak to you privately for a moment please."

Royal looked confused at first, but then said, "Sure." He followed Ramsey out into the hallway just outside of the office. "What's up?"

"Correct me if I'm mistaken, but didn't you say Gemma was at work today?"

"Yes," Royal said on high alert now thinking something had happened to his wife. "Why? What's wrong?"

Ramsey mused over his answer. "Nothing's wrong."

"Ram, you pulled me out of a meeting with a supplier, something you never do, to ask me about my wife. Level with me."

Ramsey shook his head. Frustrated. "Gianna told me she was going to be with Gemma today but how can she when Gemma's at work?"

"Gem got off work at noon. She called to tell me she was meeting Gianna for lunch."

More confusion disturbed Ramsey because, while that may have been the case, it still didn't explain where Gianna was this morning. "Okay. That explains it," he said just to end Royal's curiosity.

"Is everything okay on the home front?" Royal asked.

"Yes. I'm just trying to keep tabs on Gianna."

"You could just call her."

"I could..."

"Is she okay?"

"Yes. She's fine," Ramsey said. "I've been

extra vigilant since she's been pregnant. I don't want to keep disturbing her throughout the day with phone calls every time I think something is wrong. At the same time, I'm always worried about her."

"That's understandable," Royal said, "But Gianna's a big girl. She's carried the world on her shoulders once upon a time."

A reminiscent smile touched Ramsey's lips. "Yes, she did."

Royal glanced at his watch. "Hey, I'll take Copeland around if you want to check in with Gianna. I can pull Regal into a conference room with us to go over the materials."

"That would be great. Thanks, Royal."

When Ramsey and Royal stepped back inside of Ramsey's office, Ramsey explained the change in plans. Royal went ahead and left the office with Mr. Copeland, beginning to give him details about the Uptown project.

Ramsey closed the door to his office to call Gianna. He still had her name stored under 'Cupcake' in his contacts.

She answered, "Hey, Ramsey."

"Hey, you," Ramsey said walking away from the door, headed for the windows. "I'm feeling some kind of way over here."

"Why?"

He could hear her smiling. "You didn't call me this morning to say hi or anything. You were asleep when I left."

"I'm sorry, Ramsey. I don't want my man feeling neglected but you know I hate disturbing you at work."

"And you know I don't mind it. I really don't, Gianna. I'm not saying that just because. I mean it, baby."

"I know."

"How's my little girl?"

"She's fine."

Ramsey glanced at the clock to see the time was thirty minutes after two. "Have you eaten?"

"Yes. I had a salad and drank some lemonade."

"Did you take your prenatal vitamins?"

"I did."

"What are you up to now?"

"I'm at Gemma's house helping her decide on paint colors. She says *hi* by the way."

"Tell her I said hi." He listened as she did so and then asked yet another question. "So, you've been there all day?"

"Not the *whole* day," she responded and left it at that.

Ramsey instantly knew she was purposely withholding her whereabouts. He didn't want to pry it out of her, but it was looking like he'd have to. It would have to wait until later, though, when he could talk to her face-to-face. Read her.

"Well, I gotta go, sweetie. I have some pressing matters here that I need to take care of. I'll see you when I get home, okay."

"Okay, Ramsey."

"I love you."

"I love you, too."

He slid his phone back into his pocket, shook his head in confusion and left the office, looking for Royal and Mr. Copeland.

# Chapter 5

Watching Carson cook was better than relaxing to a movie while eating over-buttered popcorn with her feet propped up, Gianna concluded. His buttermilk fried chicken tasted better than any chicken she'd ever had at a restaurant and she couldn't wait to get her hands on a few pieces.

Waiting for some cupcakes to cool before frosting, she said, "If I watch you long enough, I'd know your recipe, Carson."

The old man looked amused. "You think so, madam?"

"Yes. I can already smell the spices you used."

"Which are?"

"Hmm...let's see." She sniffed the aroma in the kitchen. "Paprika, onion powder, salt and pepper—of course—garlic powder...maybe some chili powder..."

"You're on the right track but there's a lot more than that."

"Really?"

"Yes, and then there's that secret ingredient that only I possess, madam."

"And what's that?"

"It's called, the magic touch."

Gianna laughed. "Is that right?"

"Indeed. You have that *touch* with those cupcakes of yours but with this chicken, I am the king."

Gianna laughed some more. "So, in other words, I need to stay in my lane."

"You're a quick learner, madam." Carson chuckled.

"Okay I gotcha, Carson." Gianna began icing the dozen butter pecan cupcakes that she'd made Ramsey for dessert. He didn't request any – she just wanted to make some for him. Because she loved him and seeing him happy pleased her.

"Say, what kind of operation are we running up in here?"

Gianna's face brightened in surprise when she heard Ramsey's voice. "Ramsey!" She rose to her tiptoes and still it was a struggle to get her arms around his neck, but when she finally did, Ramsey swooped down and took a kiss – a deep, toe-curling one that left her moaning – her love sounds harmonizing with the sizzle of frying chicken.

"How are you my love?" he asked after he'd gotten enough – well, enough for now.

"I'm good—making your favorite dessert."

"You're my favorite dessert," he said then pressed his lips to hers again, briefly this time. He glanced over at Carson. "You got it smelling good in here, Carson."

"Always, Sir."

Ramsey turned his attention to Gianna again when he said, "Hold that enthusiasm. I'm going to go up and change. I'll be right back."

"Okay."

He proceeded up the stairs arriving at the second level where he keyed in the entry code for the third-floor master bedroom suite. Gianna's whereabouts this morning still nagged him. He wasn't the kind of guy that needed to know every move his wife made but he at least wanted the assurance that she would be where she said she would. What if there was an emergency? What if she needed him?

After changing into sweats and a T-shirt that showed off a portion of his hairy chest, Ramsey jogged downstairs and asked, "How much longer before dinner's ready, Carson?"

"About a half hour, Sir."

"Okay. Gianna, if you need me, I'll be in the office for a few."

"Okay."

Ramsey sauntered there with Gianna still heavy on his mind. Sitting behind his desk now, he slid on his glasses and logged into his workstation. Regal had sent him a list of construction materials and he needed to confirm the accuracy of it before getting official quotes from Glasgow so they could know what kind of prices to expect. Even still, he found it difficult to focus, and he knew he wouldn't be able to until he had a real talk with Gianna over dinner.

\* \* \*

Midway through dinner, after she'd had

three pieces of buttermilk chicken, Ramsey decided to come right out and ask, "Gianna, where did you go when you left the house this morning?"

Gianna smiled and playfully narrowed her eyes. "Why are you always trying to keep tabs on me?"

"Not always." Ramsey took a sip of red wine. He set the glass on the table and continued, "But *today* I want to know where you were."

The smile fell from her face when she realized he was serious. He had that I-ain't-playing expression on his face – a look like he was just about to make some important business decision, but this evening, *she* was his business. "Why?"

"Why does it matter *why*?" Ramsey asked, testily. "Just tell me where you were. Simple as that."

Gianna took a sip of water. Dang. She'd been caught, yet again. Could she do anything without him knowing about it?

"The fact that you're taking so long to answer me is really starting to bother me, Gianna."

"That's only because I don't want to tell you where I was."

"Is there a reason for that?" he asked calmly, staring at her.

She looked back at him, held his gaze for a long time then said, "There is. I knew you would be angry and—"

Uninterested in finishing dinner, he set his plate aside, looked at Gianna and said, "Tell me."

Gianna sighed. "Okay. Um...I met Geraldine at Jetton Park this morning." She saw the moment his eyes darkened. Saw the storm brewing. Disappointment building.

"You met your mother at the park and you kept this from me?"

"Yes."

"Because you knew I'd be angry," he said repeating *her* reasoning.

"Yes, and now you are. I can feel your mood changing already."

"I asked you last night what your plans were for today. You said you were going to be at Gemma's."

"I *was* at Gemma's—"

"Yes, but not the whole day, obviously, and if you met up with your mother at the park, I'm sure this is something you two had already prearranged. Yet, you failed to let me in on those plans. Can you see why this is frustrating for me, Gianna, or is it lost on you?"

His glare thickened at her non-reply. She just sat there, rubbing her temples and avoiding eye contact with him.

"Gianna?"

"No," she finally answered. "It's not lost on me, but just know that it's really frustrating for me to have to plan stuff behind your back, Ramsey. Look what happens when you find out. You look furious right now."

"You've never seen me furious. You don't know that look. I'm more upset right now than anything else and that's because you lied to me."

"I didn't lie to you, Ramsey. I just didn't tell you where I was going."

"As far as I'm concerned that's the same thing." He frowned slightly. "For future reference, when I ask you where you are or what your plans are, I want to know everything—not bits and pieces. Do you understand?"

"Yes," Gianna replied because offering a rebuttal at this point would take more energy out of her than carrying a baby.

"And of all people, you met with Geraldine? The crazy, psycho chick whose mere presence threw you into a panic attack? *That* Geraldine? The liar? The woman who toys with people's emotions like it's one of her hobbies? The woman who left you and Gemma to fend for yourselves when you were growing up? *That* Geraldine?"

Ramsey stood up and put his hands in his pockets, pacing the floor. "Listen, I'm not trying to chastise you—"

"That's what it feels like."

He stopped pacing. Looked at her. "How else am I suppose to relay to you what I'm feeling at the moment? The fact of the matter is, you didn't tell me about this *secret* meeting because you knew I wouldn't allow it, and for good reason. What if Geraldine went nuts again and threw you into another anxiety attack?"

"That didn't happen, Ramsey."

"I know that didn't happen," he said raising his voice a pitch, "But what if it did? That's my point. And what did she want, anyway?"

"She—she wanted to apologize to me...said she wants to be a part of the baby's life."

He chuckled in disbelief. "That's not going to happen...just like you're never meeting up with the lady again."

"Ramsey—"

"You are *my* wife. *My* responsibility and that baby you're carrying is *my* responsibility."

"I know that—"

"And I thought I made myself clear to you the last time you tried to do things independently of me. It doesn't work that way anymore, Gianna. You cannot take things on your shoulders, say you'll deal with them and completely cut me out of the picture. You did that when I told you I'd make sure Gemma got to that Atlanta hospital when she was sick and you're still doing it. Stop trying so hard to fight my headship and let me have what's rightfully mine. You, your heart, your *trust*—faith that I know what's right for you. For us. I can lead this family in the right direction, but not if you're constantly working against me."

Ramsey stared at her for a moment more, then said, "That's all I have to say." He exited the room. Some things he didn't understand about women. He was all set to give Gianna the world, yet she wanted to forge her own path. It was the result of marrying a smart, strong, independent woman, he knew, but she would have to learn to trust him. There was no way around it.

# Chapter 6

Gianna was at the bakery today icing red velvet cupcakes while replaying last night's conversation with Ramsey. She couldn't concentrate. She messed up a few cupcakes and had to make more batches of cream cheese frosting. Ramsey had it all wrong. She *did* trust him. Her problem was that she still had the independent spirit about herself and she wasn't accustomed to dealing with his strong, take-charge personality as well as she should have been – at least by now. He was dominant in every way a man could display the trait. She realized he tried to turn it down for her but at times, like last night, he couldn't, especially when he felt he needed to get a point across.

This morning, she heard him get up for work, but she stayed in bed as long as she could to avoid being in his way. He finally woke her up around 8:30, the time he usually left for work. She usually left at around 9:00. Lately, 9:15. Anyway, he'd left her vitamins on the nightstand, given her a kiss and told her he loved her – the norm – but she could still feel his frustration and that made her tense. Not to mention he hadn't bothered eating a single cupcake she'd made for dessert last night.

When she heard the doorbell chime, Gianna walked from the back and saw Gemma walking into the bakery wearing a pair of black and white leggings with a long, yellow tunic. Her hair looked damp. Freckles cute. Curls poppin'. She had on a pair of silver, hoop earrings and the birthstone necklace that Gianna had purchased for her.

"Hey, sis. You look beautiful today."

"Thanks," Gemma said. "So do you."

"Please...you don't have to lie. I'm wearing a hairnet and I feel like a pack of Twinkies."

Gemma laughed. "Aw, Gianna." She walked behind the counter and gave her sister a shoulder rub. "Little sister is here to help."

"Don't you supposed to be at work?"

"I'm off today. I'm supposed to be home working on the mission statement for the Gemma Jacobsen Foundation. Shh...don't tell Royal." She giggled. "Now, what can I do? Do you need some cupcakes frosted? Tell me what you need."

"Can you make some fresh coffee?"

"Yes. Fresh coffee, coming right up." Gemma dumped the old coffee filter and started a new brew. "All done with that. What else?"

"Can you work the register for a minute? I need to take a break. My feet hurt."

"Sure, sis. Go take a load off. I got this."

"Thanks." Gianna stepped into her office, closed the door and sat at her desk literally holding her head up with her hands. Her feet didn't hurt, but her head did. She was hyper-aware of how quickly her relationship with

Ramsey had developed so quickly and became what it is now – not to say their whirlwind romance was the cause of this argument. She loved her husband, but the marriage, pregnancy, running the bakery, dealing with Geraldine and wanting to deepen her relationship with her father was all taking a toll on her physically. She definitely didn't need the stress. Having a baby was supposed to be a joyful time for parents. While she was happy, all of these changes would take some getting used to, and that was the frustrating part about all of it. She wasn't all that used to being married, to having a protector – a man at her beck and call – so how would she get used to the pregnancy, being a mother while running a business and trying to mend broken relationships with her parents?

"Hey, cupcake, you have a visitor," Gemma said peeping around the door.

Gianna's heartbeat instantly pounded harder at the thought of that visitor being Ramsey. She wasn't in the right frame of mind to talk to him right now. Her thoughts were scattered. Mind in a million places at once. Rehashing an argument and hearing Ramsey preach on and on about how it's his responsibility to do this and that would only worsen her tension headache.

"Who is it?" she finally asked.

"It's Jerry."

"Oh." *Shrew.* "Tell him to come on back."

"Okay."

Gianna sat up, took a sip of water and

attempted a series of fake smiles to mask the flustered look on her face just in time to see Jerry appear in the doorway.

"Hey, Jerry."

"Hey, daughter."

"You look nice this afternoon," she told him. He had on a pair of black jeans and a black polo. "Are you on your lunch break?"

"Yes...figured I'd swing by here to see what my only daughter was up to." Jerry had recently settled into his role as a sales associate at an auto parts store on Tryon Street, near Sugar Creek. It wasn't a lucrative job by any stretch of the imagination, but he enjoyed it.

"I'm baking my butt off—the norm. What about you? Are you enjoying working again?"

"I am. It feels good to get back out here and do something in this world. I have you and St. Claire to thank for that."

Gianna smiled. Jerry had always called Ramsey by his last name. It was Ramsey who figured out Jerry was her father. And he also bought Jerry a new wardrobe and took him to the barber to get a fresh cut.

"Are you running into any issues with the house?" Gianna inquired. Jerry was living in her house – the place she lived before she married Ramsey.

"No. Everything is still like it was."

"And you have food and everything?"

Jerry chuckled. "Now, don't you be worrying about me, sugar. You have enough to worry about right there in your belly."

Gianna rested a hand on her stomach and

smiled. "Yes, I do."

"Is everything okay with my grandbaby?"

"Yes. All is well with this little girl."

"And what about you?"

Gianna glanced up at him. "Everything is okay with me."

"Are you sure about that?" Jerry asked.

Gianna flashed a weak smile, then watched Jerry sit in the chair next to her desk.

He sighed, took a quick glance at the clock up high on the wall and said, "I never told you this, Gianna, but the reason I started coming to this bakery so frequently had nothing to do with me wanting cupcakes. Now, don't get me wrong—your cupcakes are delicious and kept me coming back for more, but I remember one of the first times I came by here. You were sitting on the floor crying your pretty little eyes out. You looked like you were in deep distress— like whatever you were going through at the time was so bad, you couldn't see your way out of it. I didn't know what to do about it. There I was, couldn't even take care of myself...what was I going to do to help you? So, I did what I could do, and that was to keep an eye on you. That's what I called myself doing—being there to make sure you were okay because you were so disturbed that day."

Gianna nodded, remembering that tumultuous time in her life.

"I say that to say this—if you need to talk to your old man, and I don't care what about, you know I'm here. I may not speak the best, but my intentions are pure."

Her weak smile was a dead giveaway of her troubles, Gianna knew, and seemed Jerry had a knack for noticing when something was bothering her.

"Now, tell me what's going on."

"Jer—"

"Ain't no need in denying it," Jerry interrupted. "I can see the trouble in your eyes."

Gianna considered all that was going on in her life and debated on which aspect of it she could share with him. She said, "It's a combination of things. Back then, I thought I was on the verge of a nervous breakdown going through all the health issues with Gemma, but now I feel just as much pressure, if not more, with the expectations of being a mother and fulfilling my role as a wife. And then Geraldine reached out to me—said she wants to be a part of the baby's life. Told me she had a drinking problem..."

"Well, she ain't lying about that. Even when we were together, she had an alcohol problem."

"Really? All those years ago?"

"She did. I tried to get her some help, but Geraldine always did what Geraldine wanted. She never took anyone else's feelings into consideration."

"Question...if she's always been that way, how did you bring yourself to love her so much, Jerry?"

Jerry paused reflectively. "The heart wants what the heart wants and boy did I fall for her. She was beautiful—still is. She didn't have much in the way of common sense, but I thought her beauty was enough to make up for the fact that she was a little cuckoo, you know. Then, I started seeing her how ugly her actions were and her beauty no longer mattered to me. She would throw tantrums if I didn't buy something she wanted or if she didn't get her way. I remember once, she took some grocery and bill money I gave her, went to the mall and bought a five-hundred-dollar purse. You tell me—what sense is there in toting around a five-hundred-dollar purse when you ain't got a *dime* to put in it?"

Gianna chuckled until tears came to her eyes.

Jerry laughed, too, then continued, "Whenever I didn't cave and give her what she wanted, she'd get to drinking."

"She told me she wants to get help."

"People can *say* whatever they want. What are they *doing* though? If you say you need to bake some cream cheese carrot cupcakes, but you sit back here in the office all day, how are the cupcakes going to get baked?"

"I see your point."

"Don't let Geraldine stress you out. Honestly, I don't trust her, and neither does St. Claire."

"How do you know that?"

"When he saw us in the parking lot that day," Jerry whistled. "He was burning mad...told Geraldine to her face she was heartless and how glad he was that you were nothing like her." Jerry stood up, keeping all kind of noises that sounded like a blend of yawns and old-age screeches.

"You gotta go?"

"Yeah, better be getting back to the job before the boss man comes looking for me."

"Wait." Gianna got up from her desk and walked to the kitchen where she picked up a half-dozen, packaged cupcakes and handed the box to him just like old times.

Jerry pulled out his wallet.

"What are you doing?" she asked.

He took out a ten-dollar bill and said, "I'm working now, sweet thang. I can afford to buy them."

"You know you don't have to, Jerry."

"I want to," he said, handing her the money. "Take it."

"Jerry—"

"I insist."

Gianna took the money only because he persisted. "Thank you."

"Thank *you*. Have a good day, daughter."

"You, too, Jerry." She smiled as he walked away.

# Chapter 7

Things between Ramsey and Gianna remained tense.

Ramsey was suited impeccably, dressed to the nines for work again, standing next to the bed *again*, looking at Gianna before he woke her up. And when he did wake her, he gave her a kiss on the lips today before jogging downstairs. He took his coffee along with a ham and cheese bagel to-go instead of having his morning chat with Carson.

Sitting at his desk looking at the Paris sketch again, he pulled his glasses away from his face and rubbed his eyes. Around the same time, Judy came inside.

"Here's your coffee, Sir. I took the liberty of putting it in a thermos since you have an off-site meeting this morning."

Brows furrowed, he asked, "An off-site meeting where?" He scrambled to look at his calendar.

"At the University City apartments with Ralph Sheppard."

"How did I forget that?" he asked, but he knew how. His days had been off since he and Gianna weren't exactly meshing. He glanced at his watch. It was already a quarter past ten.

"I'll call Ralph and let him know you're running behind."

"Thanks, Judy." Ramsey took the thermos from his desk and headed to the elevator. He was one of those people who took pride in practicing what he preached. He was punctual and expected the same from his employees. He wasn't one of those do-as-I-say-not-as-I-do bosses. He led by example. So for him to be late for anything, even a simple site meeting, had him upset with himself.

At least the site wasn't that far away. St. Claire Architects was located on IBM Drive, and since the completion of the new overpass over I-85 that connected IBM Drive to Ikea Boulevard, he arrived at the apartment site on University City Boulevard in less than ten minutes.

"Please excuse my tardiness," he told Ralph as soon as he exited the truck.

"No worries, Sir. I was sitting here eating breakfast and looking at all the businesses going up around here. It's amazing. Outback is here now. A Starbucks just opened, Culver's, and I hear they're building a fancy, new Mexican restaurant over there."

"Yeah. This area has seen an explosion of growth over the last six months." Ramsey looked around, taking in the landscaping of the apartment complex. Already he saw something that made his temple pulsate. Did Ralph see it, too? "What were your concerns about the landscaping again?"

"It wasn't necessarily that I had any

concerns, Sir. I wanted you to take a look at the new landscaping features CitySites added to this building compared to work they've done for us in the past."

"Right." Ramsey dropped his hands into his pockets, annoyed that Ralph—a project manager—didn't pick up on the brown grass. Why was there brown grass? This was a luxury apartment building. The grass was supposed to be green. Lustrous. Not brown and depressing. Maybe it was a small detail to some, but not to him.

"Take a look at the tropical plants. Keep in mind CitySites are scheduled to return and plant the spring plants in a few weeks. I also had them line the sidewalk for the leasing office entrance with perennials. What do you think?"

"I like the perennials and the tropical plants give the place personality and style, for sure, but what's up with the brown grass?"

"That, I'm not sure about but I can check with Craig."

"You do that. I pay top dollar for premium grass, so I want grass that stays green all year round. I never want to roll up to one of our properties and see brown grass."

"Yes, Sir. I'll get right on that as soon as I'm back at the office."

The men took a full lap around the structure. Besides the grass issue, the rest of the landscaping was up to Ramsey's standards. "It's certainly a change from the norm, but I like what they did here. All I need you to do is take care of the grass issue for me and if they give you any pushback, get Royal on it. I'm going to be away for the rest of the day."

"All right, Sir. Thanks for swinging by."

"No problem," Ramsey told him. "I won't be late next time."

\* \* \*

Ramsey left the site heading outbound on Tryon Street towards JW Clay Boulevard – destination – his woman. He made a left on J M Keynes Drive, found a park near the bakery and got out walking with purpose for the door. He nodded at a few people as he approached. When he pulled the handle to the entrance, the aroma of the place hit him – smelled like chocolate, cinnamon and sweetness. He glanced at the chalkboard on the wall seeing the cupcake of the day – the banana cream cupcake – then he looked at the drink display fridge. It was stocked with milk and water. The coffee was made, the 'open' sign illuminated and the tip jar was displayed on the counter. It was quiet inside except for the rattling of pans in the back and the soft music coming from the speakers. Most of the bakery's morning customers were just in and out, grabbing coffee and a cupcake on the way to their various jobs. That was good for Gianna – it would give her time to do more uninterrupted baking. However, Ramsey didn't like the fact that she was in the back while she had customers sitting out in the front.

He took a seat at his usual table and waited to see how long it would be before she made an appearance. He knew she heard the bell. So, where was she?

He got his answer when he saw her walk to the front wearing a logo embroidered apron and a hairnet. She looked at him – just looked – not showing any sort of emotion. Without him having to ask, she fixed him a large cup of coffee and took a banana cream cupcake from the display case then began walking over to him. While she was headed his way, she couldn't escape the heat of his deliberate stare, nor could she pretend she didn't feel the extra breaths escape her lungs or the way her heart drummed in her chest just by the sight of her husband. He was hers and she took great pride in knowing that. Still, there were things about him that would take some getting used to.

"Hi, Ramsey." She set the coffee and cupcake on the table in front of him.

Ramsey, analyzing her, didn't like the look on her face. Normally, whenever she saw him, especially at the bakery, she'd smile. This time, she kept a straight face and the warm demeanor that was typical of her was nowhere to be found.

"Gianna?"

"Yes?" she asked as she walked toward the counter.

"Can you come back over here for a minute?"

"Ramsey, I have cupcakes in the oven," she said in an exasperated breath.

"Okay, then come back after you take them out."

Gianna continued on to the back, took the vanilla cupcakes from the oven, then put in some chocolate ones. She immediately headed back for Ramsey because she knew if she hadn't, he would be back there with her.

As she neared the table, he reached out for her and so instead of sitting, she walked over to him and stood between his long, opened legs as he folded his arms around her, his head touching her stomach. And then he looked up at her.

Smiled.

So did she, her hands gliding across the wool texture of his beard, and then she traced his lips with her index finger.

"We need to talk," he said his lips moving against her fingers.

"We do," she agreed.

"Do you have a minute?"

"Yes." She took the seat across from him.

Ramsey took a sip of coffee, but his gaze never left her.

"You look especially GQ today," she told him. "You must've had an important meeting."

"I did. I'm scheduled to meet with my wife today. You may know her. She's beautiful. She has the prettiest eyes, luxurious brown hair and she always smells like cupcakes."

Gianna smiled small, almost like his words didn't have a ring of believability to them.

Ramsey peeped that and said further, "I remember all the times I sat here, waiting for you and when you would look up to see me, your face would light up with the biggest, prettiest smile. Today, you saw me and there was nothing. No smile. No glow. You just looked at me."

"I know. I...uh...I have so many things on my mind, Ramsey."

"So much that you can't give me a smile?"

"Well, we aren't exactly seeing eye-to-eye these days."

"Because of your secret meeting with Geraldine," Ramsey said.

"No. Because of your *response* when you found out about the meeting, Ramsey. You lost it."

"I didn't *lose* it, sweetheart. I went into protective mode. I tried to explain that to you at dinner the other night, Gianna. It's highly unsettling for me to think about you being alone with Geraldine. I don't trust the woman. She abandoned you. She left you to raise Gemma on your own. Kept your father a secret for years. You poured your heart out to this woman and all she did was sip cappuccino and cross her legs like she didn't have a care in the world. And look at us—even now, we have this rift between us because of her."

"It's not only that, Ramsey. I—"

A customer walked in just as Gianna was about to make an attempt to explain herself and her feelings. She looked at Ramsey. "How long can you stay?"

"I'm free for the rest of the day, so I can stay til' whenever."

"Okay. Let me go take care of her. I'll be right back."

Gianna rung up the lady's order – a medium coffee and the cupcake of the day. She paid and went on her way, then Gianna rejoined Ramsey at the table. "As I was saying, I feel like everything I do, I have to run it by you for your approval."

Ramsey shook his head. "You don't, Gianna, but when I ask you what your plans are and you purposely don't tell me, that's a problem. What if this meeting with your mother went to the left? What if you had a panic attack? That's not what happened, thank God, but I'm always trying to think ahead, baby. I know I can be overbearing at times but you—Gianna—you're my life. My everything. Without you, I cease to exist."

Gianna frowned. "Don't say that."

"It's true." Ramsey took a moment to think about her and how much she meant to him. She could get to him in ways other people couldn't. She had access to his heart, and he knew she was the key to his happiness. He reached across the table, held her warm hand in his and said, "I'm in love with you."

Gianna smiled nervously.

"I am. I don't know how to soften that. I don't *want* to soften it. I want to love you with all of my heart. Protect you." He squeezed her hand. "I would do anything for you, Gianna. You know that, don't you?"

"Yes, Ramsey."

"Then, let me."

A smile of appreciation beautified her face. "Okay. I'm sorry I kept the meeting with

Geraldine a secret from you."

"And I'm sorry reacted the way I did. It's just something about the woman that rubs me the wrong way."

"*Everything* about her rubs me the wrong way," Gianna said, then giggled. "But, she said she has a drinking problem and wants to get help."

"Do you believe her?"

Gianna shrugged. "Don't know. Jerry came by here yesterday. I mentioned it to him just to see what he thought about it."

"What was his take on it?"

"He doesn't trust anything she says."

"I'm with him on that." Ramsey released Gianna's hand, then sipped more coffee. "How is he doing by the way?"

"He's good, I think. He looked good." Gianna smiled. "He actually paid me for his cupcakes."

"I'd say that's progress."

"Me too," she said smiling, holding Ramsey's dark gaze for a moment, then shying away from him.

"I know you have to get back to work," Ramsey said. "We'll talk later, okay?"

"Okay, Ramsey."

Ramsey stood tall, all six-feet-five of pure, unfiltered male. He extended his hand to her, encouraging her to grasp it as he helped her stand. He closed his arms around her again, gave a gentle squeeze, then looked down at her, cradling her face in his right palm. He lowered his mouth to hers, kissed her softly, before seeking the taste of her tongue, clinging to it with his. Any more force and he'd consume it, and her, in one hungry, appetizing session. Since she had to finish off her workday, he'd get all he could and hope it would hold him over until she got home.

And so he lost his tongue in her mouth's recesses and sucked on her tongue until he had the full flavor of it, right along with her lips. He heard her moans. Ate them. He felt her body quiver. It turned him on. For a split second, he'd forgotten they were at the bakery until he heard the doorbell chime. He suctioned his lips away from hers and whispered, "We'll resume this later."

"Okay," she said, seemingly spellbound, lost in his eyes.

He ran his thumb across her lips. "Don't work too hard today."

"I won't. Bye, Ramsey."

"See you later, baby."

And just like that, marital beef was squashed, the sun beamed brighter and all was right with the world. Gianna watched him walk away, completely enamored just by his signature walk alone. He was the whole package and she couldn't wait to go home to open it.

# Chapter 8

He could have had someone do it for him – pick out the freshest bouquet of red roses, but he went to the florist on his own and chose the perfect bouquet for his lady. With his kind of money, a jeweler would happily show up at his house, but he took the initiative to drive to the jeweler – the same one he'd purchased their wedding rings from – to purchase a gift for Gianna. He saw several pieces he wanted to buy for her, but knowing Gianna, she'd be overwhelmed with too much all at once. He settled on a two-carat, three stone drop diamond pendant. He could picture her wearing it already.

For dinner, he'd instructed Carson to cook shrimp, lobster and steak prepared any way he wanted it. While Carson cooked, Ramsey situated candles on the dining room table, turned on some smooth R&B then shot the breeze with Carson in the kitchen until he heard the moment Gianna came in the front door. He sprang into action, taking the bouquet of roses to the door.

"Welcome home, baby. These are for you," he said, handing her the roses, but she didn't take them.

Gianna covered her mouth with both hands in sheer excitement and surprise.

Ramsey smiled. Every time he bought her something – no matter how big or small – surprise and shock took over her features. Like when he surprised her with a yearly membership for massages, or when he gave her a bag of plain M&Ms. "Ramsey, they're beautiful," she said.

"Not as beautiful as my breathtaking wife who smells like cupcakes right now," he said embracing her with his face buried in her neck, taking deep inhales of her scent.

He released her then gave her a peck on the lips.

"You're going to make me cry," she said, her eyes already tearing up.

"Don't cry, baby."

She fanned her eyes, withholding the emotion. "Thank you for the roses."

"You're welcome."

Gianna heard the soft music playing, smelled seafood and why was Ramsey all dressed up, even more dapper now than when she saw him earlier?

"Ramsey, why'd you change suits?"

"I wanted to look as fly as possible for my queen."

"You look fly in just about anything you wear, especially those boxer briefs that cling to you just right."

Ramsey nibbled on his lip. "Keep that up and we'll forgo everything I planned for you tonight and head straight to the bedroom."

"You've planned something for me?"

"Yes. First, step out of those shoes," he urged.

Gianna took off her shoes, left them by the door and then took Ramsey's waiting hand. He led her to the candlelit dining room where she saw food already on the table – a feast fit for a king – lobster, shrimp, steak and a fancy salad. And then there were buttered rolls, corn on the cob and creamy mashed potatoes.

"Wow. What is all of this, Ramsey?"

"A special dinner for us. I mean, all of our dinners are special, but I think we've been a little stressed lately, so tonight we'll take our time, discuss a few things and enjoy ourselves over some good food."

A smile came to Gianna's face – one Ramsey delighted to see. He pulled out her chair and confirmed her comfort before he sat down. He fanned out a cloth napkin, spread it in her lap.

"I feel so underdressed," she said as her eyes traced the precision cut of his beard. "You went to the barber, too."

"I did. I know how you can't get enough of this beard. I figured I'd enhance it for you."

Gianna touched his face, feeling the firmness of his jaw beneath her hand. She smiled, thoroughly pleased.

Ramsey reached for the bread as Carson stepped into the room.

"Hey, Carson," Gianna told him.

"Good evening, madam." He served her a sample of the food, set the plate in front of her, then proceeded to prepare a plate for Ramsey.

"Thank you, Carson. You've really gone above and beyond tonight."

"That's why you pay me the big bucks, Sir."

Ramsey cracked a smile, then after Carson left the room, he looked at Gianna until his stare prompted her to look back at him. "Let's eat."

Gianna went for the shrimp first, savoring the flavor of it. Carson was an excellent cook. He was talented at everything he did.

When Ramsey saw Gianna tearing into the shrimp, he asked, "How is it?"

"Oh my goodness," she mumbled. "It's so good. I didn't realize how hungry I was."

"Well, you are eating for two."

"Right," she said.

Ramsey ate a chunk of butter-dipped lobster then said, "So, first on the agenda—"

Her loud moans while eating the shrimp disrupted his thoughts. He looked at her and watched her stuff another shrimp into her mouth, chasing it with a spoon full of mashed potatoes.

Gianna stopped chewing when she glanced up at him and caught his gaze. Embarrassed, she covered her mouth with her hand. "Sorry..."

Ramsey's eyes crinkled in the corners. "It's fine, Gianna. My girls have to eat, right?"

She nodded, steadily chewing.

"As I was saying, first on the agenda is the bakery. In roughly two months, our little girl will be here. Have you thought about how long you're going to take off work?"

Gianna held up a finger, took a long sip of water then responded, "Not sure. I was thinking three months, but I already can't imagine going back to work and leaving my little cupcake behind, even after we've bonded."

"I know, and you probably won't, so where does that leave us?"

Gianna sighed. "Since I haven't made up my mind, let's just plan for three months and whatever happens up to that three-month mark, we'll deal with it then."

Ramsey smiled. "That sounds like something I would say. You've been hanging around me too long."

"I think that's the other way around, Mr. St. Claire."

Ramsey served himself more mashed potatoes. "Whatever you—we—decide to do, we're going to have to hire someone to help you at the bakery. There's no way around it. We've been talking about it for a while, but now it's to the point where we can't put it off any longer. That's why I had my secretary put out some ads."

"You did?"

"Yes."

"When?"

Ramsey didn't see the relevancy of the question but still, he answered, "Not long ago, and we already have a good number of applicants. I was thinking we could hire a college student part-time to work the register and someone else you can train for the baking portion of the job."

"That sounds good."

Ramsey raised his brows. "Excuse me?"

"What?"

"I'm astounded you don't have any objections."

"Nope. Not one. I'm going with the flow," Gianna said.

"Then, moving right along, we need to talk about a nanny."

"Uh...no we don't."

Ramsey chuckled. "What happened to *going with the flow*?"

"We don't need a nanny, Ramsey."

Amused, Ramsey asked, "Why do you look so serious all of a sudden?"

"Because I *am* serious. I'm so anti-nanny."

"You're *anti-nanny*?" he repeated, so tickled, he could hardly get the words out. "May I ask why you're...um...anti-nanny?"

"I've seen enough movies to know that hiring a nanny spells disaster. Either this *nanny* person is going to turn all psycho and try to kidnap my baby, or give you google eyes and hint that she could be better for you than me."

Ramsey threw his head back with laughter. "Oh, my sweet Gianna. Did you say *google* eyes?" He laughed some more.

"You laugh, but I'm serious. You're too hot to be having some woman around constantly playing mommy on a daily basis, checking you out. Wishing..."

"You've been watching too many movies, woman. And here I was thinking it was Gemma who was addicted to movies."

"Are you under the assumption that things like that don't happen in real life?"

Ramsey wiped his mouth and said, "I'm sure they do, but any outsider I bring in the house will be fully vetted all the way down to their social media posts. And as for another woman giving me *googly* eyes, if that happens, I wouldn't be aware of it. I only have eyes for you, sweetness."

"Really?"

"Yes, really," he said, his posture relaxed, still somewhat tickled by her.

"Even though I look all puffy?" Gianna grinned.

"If you think you look puffy, it's definitely all in your head. You're all stomach and I love it. I love the way you look. The pounds you've gained. I put that baby inside of you. Why wouldn't I love it, and you? Make no mistake, Gianna—I gave you my name and I am one-hundred percent dedicated to you. That should never be a question."

Gianna smiled, flooded with warmth.

"Let's put the nanny subject on ice for now and talk about the layout of the house instead."

Ramsey reached for the steak when he saw Gianna making an attempt to get the tray. He served her a piece.

"Thanks."

"Welcome." He watched her eat for a moment and smiled. Nibbled his lip. The littlest things she did made him want her, and she wasn't even aware.

"The layout," she said, reminding him of what he wanted to discuss next.

"Ah, yes," he said, breaking his trance. "Our room is on the third floor. There are two rooms available on the second floor, but I wouldn't want the baby down there alone."

"Me either, although, it would only be an issue at night when we're in our room."

"Yep." Ramsey ate some salad. Thought for a moment. "We could do some work to fix the third floor, like adding an extra room."

Her eyes bulged. "You'd do that?"

"I'll do whatever's necessary."

"But that would involve construction? This house is large enough as it is." Gianna narrowed her eyes as she tried to come up with a solution.

"What are you thinking?" he asked.

"As a short-term solution, maybe we should set up the crib in our room. We could even use some room dividers to make a designated area for the baby, then as she gets older, we can slowly transition her to the nursery on the second floor."

Ramsey nodded. "We can give that a try."

"Cool."

"See what we can accomplish with teamwork?"

"Yes, and it also helps when your husband is a genius."

"Finish your food, woman, so I can take you upstairs, and when I say take you upstairs I mean *take* you upstairs."

Her cheeks reddened.

"I love how flustered you get when I talk like this to you. We've made love too many times to count, and I still have the ability to make you blush."

"I don't think that will ever change," Gianna admitted.

"You don't want it to change do you?" he asked, lightly stroking his fork down the length of her forearm, then bringing the fork to his mouth, pretending to eat.

She glanced over at him and saw the intentional smile on his face, but along with it, she felt the vibes between them – the heat. The love.

# Chapter 9

Gianna undressed and stepped inside of the stand-up shower, feeling the warm water massage her tired body. Before bed, this was the routine for her and tonight wasn't the exception. She especially needed it after being on her feet all day at the bakery. She closed her eyes while the water rained down on her hair and when her strands were fully saturated, she threw her head back, opened her eyes again and screamed.

Ramsey was standing just outside the glass doors like a shadow, completely naked and waiting.

"Ramsey!" Gianna panted, her heart beating so fast, it threw her breathing pattern off. "How—how long have you been standing there?"

"Too long," he said, opening the door, joining her in the shower, immediately drawing her close to him, so close that his thickness was pressed snugly against her midsection.

Gianna placed kisses on his thick pecs, enjoying his hairy chest before looking up into his eyes as warm water connected their souls. Something else was about to deepen that connection – something only he could give her.

They were about to heat things up even more and it had nothing to do with the water's temperature.

He took her mouth with enough skill and precision to immediately steal her tongue and she reciprocated by taking his, moaning desperately, feeling his hands grip and squeeze her backside. Feelings of submission – of letting go and freeing herself to all the love he had to give – immediately took over her mind. And then she heard the primitive groans he made, indicating his need was a raw, potent one. His groans alone made her body temperature soar a few degrees.

He temporarily broke the connection with her mouth to savor her neck. His lips grazed her breasts, sucked water from their peaks before he lowered himself to his knees, painted kisses on her stomach before resting his head there. Water rained down on him and he stayed there, on his knees. Face to belly. Hands still on her backside. Bonding. Absorbing love. Bathing in joy. Drowning in desire.

Without warning, he touched her most intimate spot. Made her gasp. Made her legs shake, then he quickly stood up to stabilize her.

"You okay?" he asked, reading her. Drops of water fell from the tip of his nose. Water drenched his hair and beard.

"Yes, I'm okay," she said, breathless.

"Then, why did your whole body jump when I touched you here?" he asked, reaching to touch her *there* yet again with his middle finger.

For a second time, her body shook. Pleasure quaked through her. "I guess I'm just super-sensitive." She swallowed hard. "I heard that was—um—normal during pregnancy."

He deliberately fiddled with her femininity, playing her like an instrument while staring at her face, watching her attempt to control the pleasure he was delivering. He saw the moment she lost herself. Saw the blush creep over her face. Studied how her eyes closed. Saw a grimace. One of pleasure, not pain. She gasped. Moaned. Bit down on her lip. Gasped some more. Her fingers twitched as she held on to his wet, hairy arms.

"Ram—Ramsey," she uttered in a soft, vacillating breath.

He took the moment to connect their mouths – suctioning her bottom lip into his mouth while still looking at her possessively, then closed his eyes and went for the whole shebang – both lips, tongue, her whole mouth – kissing her hungrily while holding her steady between his muscular arms. He took a few steps back until his legs made contact with the built-in, tiled bench in the corner of the shower. He sat down, prompting her to straddle him. He carefully held on to her while she lowered herself to the size of him. Her legs circled around his waist as he filled her. Stretched her. Stretched some more. Filled her cave to capacity and then some.

She gasped.

He groaned.

She gasped more. Her nails automatically

dug into his shoulders.

Their visions held for a moment after he was completely embedded inside of her – to the hilt with nowhere else to go although he could've gone further. He absorbed the feeling of being connected to her this way. He squeezed warm, wet flesh. She rocked her hips. He grazed her neck with his teeth. Circled his tongue in different spots. Licked water from her lips. Sucked on her tongue. Kissed her. He pulled back to see her face. He loved to see her in the heat of passion, on the verge of falling off of the cliff. He was right behind her. Falling.

"My sweet Gianna," he whispered in a way that made her eyes instantly connect with his. "You don't know what you do to me," he told her. He captured her lips, tasting her sweetness. He felt the way her body squeezed him, released then squeezed again. He liked it. He tightened his arms around her, maintaining a closer fit, then whispered how much she turned him on as the tension inside of her collided with the mounting pressure building inside of him until she erupted the same time he did, making their own waves in the shower.

She screamed.

He wouldn't let go.

She held on. More screams followed.

He still wouldn't let go.

Arms around his neck, she touched her face to his, stroking his beard with her nose then kissed his wet lips briefly. She looked at him. Smiled. "I'm in love with you," she panted. Every time they kissed, touched, made love or eye contact, she fell deeper.

"I'm in love with you, too, sweetness."

Water sprayed down on them while they stayed intimately linked together. Mind, body, spirit. As close as a man and woman could get.

"I don't want to let you go," he admitted.

"Then, don't let me go," she told him kissing him all over again.

Ramsey was more than willing to go for seconds.

# Chapter 10

Golf on acres of freshly cut, green grass is what Ramsey's Friday consisted of. He was playing good, too – ahead of Regal by five strokes, but the men weren't completely tracking scores. They both enjoyed the sport and sometimes used it to entertain some of St. Claire Architect's clients. It was something they did at least once a month, and now that the weather was getting warmer, Ramsey was sure they'd add more golf days to their agendas.

"What's your gut instinct regarding the location for the Paris project?" Regal asked. "Do you think Basile will like it?"

"He liked it on the map," Ramsey said, "But it could be a different story in person, I suppose." Ramsey got his stance right, preparing to take a swing. He whacked the ball, then behind a pair of Aviators, he stared off into the distance to see where the ball landed. "From what I know about Basile thus far is, he's picky. He wants what he wants and for the amount of money he's paying us, he deserves to *get* what he wants."

"Absolutely," Regal said. He took a swing, then the men grabbed bags, hopped in the golf cart and rode down the course.

"What have you been up to lately?" Ramsey asked Regal. "The only time I see you nowadays is at the office."

"Well, I can't stop by the house as frequently as I used to, especially now that you're married. I don't want to walk in on something."

Ramsey chuckled. "You're not going to."

"Who are you kidding, Ram? You can't keep your eyes or *hands* off of Gianna."

Ramsey smiled thinking about how true that was.

"And I'm not trying to walk up in your crib to find Gianna spread eagle on the dining room table with you holding a spoon in one hand and some cupcake frosting in the other."

Ramsey erupted in laughter. "You're funny."

"Now that you and Royal are whipped, I guess I'll have to start hanging out with Romulus."

"Yeah, good luck with that," Ramsey said, slowing the cart to a stop. They both got off. "Romulus already has a permanent kickin'-it buddy."

"Oh, true."

"And he ain't breaking his plans with Siderra for nobody."

"I imagine they'll be married next, huh," Regal said.

"Not according to Romulus. Siderra is just a friend, he says, yet she can't make a move without him knowing about it."

Regal studied the hole, then took a swing. "Yep. They'll be married next. When it happens, remember, I called it."

Ramsey chuckled. As stubborn as Romulus was he doubted if marriage was for him, but stranger things have happened. After all, he never thought he'd get married again then Gianna came along. "While we're on the subject of marriage, when are you going to take the leap?"

"I'm not," Regal responded. "My life is good as a bachelor. I can't have a woman wrecking my flow."

"So a woman would interrupt your life is what you're saying."

"Ab-so-freakin'-lutely, and I don't need any interruptions."

Ramsey shook his head. "I'm sure Wedded Bliss could find you a woman who wouldn't be too much of an interruption. In fact, I've noticed you've taken a liking to the woman who runs it."

Regal's forehead scrunched up. He lowered his dark sunglasses when he asked, "Who are you talking about? WB?"

Ramsey smirked. "Her name is Felicity James."

"Nah, Ram." Regal pushed his sunglasses back into position to cover his eyes. "I told you before—she's not my type."

"Then why are you always picking on her? Teasing her?"

"Because she's an easy target. She can't handle me."

"That's what *you* think."

"No, that's what I *know*. Can't no woman lock your boy down."

Ramsey laughed into the air. "You're in denial, Regal, if you think there isn't a woman out there who can handle you."

"Look, just because you got a lil' cupcake beauty—"

"Wait, timeout...did you say booty or beauty?"

Regal chuckled. "I said *beauty*, but ay, since Gianna's pregnant, we all know you got the—"

"Shut up, Regal. We're talking about you, not me. So, back to Felicity...she's a hard-working, black woman. An entrepreneur. I think she's just what you need."

"Sure you would, but only because your wife has her own business."

"True, but I'm not suggesting you find a woman like Felicity worthy of a shot because she has her own business. I'm merely suggesting that women as such should be looked at as valuable. The world places more value on women's physical traits. Who would've ever thought strippers would be looked at as more valuable and worthy of marriage than an entrepreneur with a good head on her shoulders? It could be just me, but there's nothing sexier than a woman who goes after what she wants and isn't afraid to be brave."

"Hey, it's pretty brave to get on a stage in a room full of men and take off your clothes, man. Give the strippers some credit."

Ramsey shook his head. "You're a strong man, Regal, but you avoid strong women."

"How would you know?"

"I know everything."

"Oh. Right...because you're *Ramsey the Great*."

Ramsey chuckled. "Don't deflect. Why is that Regal?"

"I'm not sure what you mean," Regal said when he knew exactly what his brother was hinting at.

"Okay, well you continue playing dumb, no pun intended, and I'll continue whipping your butt at this game."

"Don't for a second think you got this in the bag. They call me the comeback kid."

"Who's *they*?" Ramsey asked, mildly amused.

"Don't worry about all that. Just prepare for a last-minute upset."

"If you say so, man."

# Chapter 11

It was close to 3:00 p.m. when Gianna finally got a chance to sit down and eat her lunch – a turkey club with a side of potato salad. Felicity had brought her the food and stayed to help out around the bakery. As usual for a Friday, the place was pretty busy. There weren't any vacant tables. Some people had laptops. Others, books and cell phones. They all had coffee and cupcakes.

"G, you got a full house out here, girl," Felicity said standing at the entrance of Gianna's office.

Gianna looked up at her. Felicity was dressed cute as usual, wearing a black and white striped skirt with a denim shirt and a pair of gold flats. "That's a good thing," Gianna said garbling a mouthful of food.

"I bet if Ramsey knew you were just now eating, he'd be the one having a baby."

Gianna chuckled. "I know. He's particular that way. He puts my prenatal vitamins on the nightstand every morning."

"That's pretty, freakin' awesome."

Gianna was sipping water. She placed the bottle on the desk and said, "I know. He's just sweet that way. I just don't want him to worry so much, though."

"You can't stop a man like Ramsey St. Claire from doing what he wants to do. If he's going to worry, he's going to worry...simple as that. You could try *telling* him not to, but let's be real Gianna—the man was completely smitten with you before you were pregnant. Now, you're carrying RTG junior—"

"RTG junior?"

"Yes. Ramsey The Great, Junior."

Gianna chuckled. "I'm having a girl. Girls can't be juniors."

"Yeah, but they can be *great*."

"I can't argue with that," Gianna said. She took a bite of her sandwich.

"And I swear Ramsey gives off vibes when he's near you—like some sort of weird, uncontrollable euphoria takes over his being anytime you're around. That's only going to increase. So, let the man worry. You can't stop him."

"You're probably right."

"Ain't no probably in it. I *am* right. How's my little tater tot doing, by the way?"

Gianna smiled, knowing Felicity was talking about the baby. "She's good. The doctor says she thinks she's bigger than what she should be at this stage, though, but she didn't seem overly concerned about it...just said my due date could be a little off."

"Probably so or it could just mean she's going to be a tall girl like her daddy."

"Exactly. My own child is going to be taller than me." Gianna shook her head.

Felicity grinned. "How's the rest of the fam?"

"They're doing good. Gemma and Royal are going strong. They are so cute together."

"They are," Felicity agreed. "I'm so happy for Gemma."

"Me, too. And talk about being overprotective—girl, Royal has Gemma on his radar twenty-four-seven," Gianna said.

"Good. At least you have the assurance that he ain't going to let anything happen to his precious Gem."

"That's for certain." Gianna took another bite of her sandwich.

"What's the latest on baby shower plans?"

"There are none yet. I have to talk to Bernadette on Sunday about it. I'll have her call you to help coordinate it."

"Please do. The mother-in-law shouldn't have first dibs when it comes to the baby shower. Doesn't she know you have a best friend? Is she not aware that I exist?"

"Oh, she knows. I'm sure she can still recall you and Regal going back and forth at my marriage celebration."

Felicity smiled, then waved it off. "Nobody was paying us any attention." Gianna leaned over in the chair laughing.

"Yes, they were. I still can't believe you gave Regal a Rice Krispies as a peace offering."

"If only I could use my powers for good."

Gianna had an inkling that Felicity may have liked Regal more than she led on, but she never came out and said it. "Hey, next time I see Regal, I'll tell him you said, hi."

"No, don't do that," Felicity said. "He already told me he would come by Wedded Bliss so I can find him a wife. I don't want you making him recall that."

Gianna giggled. "He's full of it. Regal doesn't want a wife, but he does like you."

"How you figure?"

"Oh, come on, Felicity. Y'all can't get along, yet every time you're close to each other, you can't keep your eyes off of one another."

"Not true."

"Oh, yes it is," Gianna said. "If I'm not mistaken, I saw you giving him google eyes."

Felicity laughed. "Did you say *google* eyes?"

"Yep, and don't deny it."

Felicity was still laughing. "Let me go back to the front. I think I heard the bell."

Gianna giggled. "I didn't hear a bell."

"I did. *Ding, dong*," Felicity said, amused. "Did you hear it that time?"

"Whatever, Felicity." Gianna finished her water, then resumed the task of checking inventory. She already had a list of items she needed to order – milk, sugar, cups, plates, coffee – seemed she was running low on everything these days, the result of having a profitable bakery. And it was all thanks to Ramsey.

Just thinking about him must have made him think of her because now, her phone was ringing and she knew it was him calling.

"Hey," she answered.

"Hey, beautiful. You're not working too hard, are you?"

A warm sensation flooded her body. "Not really. Felicity is here. She's working the register. I have the last batch of cupcakes in the oven for one of my catering orders and while they're baking, I'm doing inventory."

"Don't worry about the inventory, baby. I'll take care of it tonight. I want you to relax."

"But you've had a long week too, Ramsey. I want *you* to relax."

"I'll relax when all of your needs are met."

"Ramsey—"

"All of them. Listen to me—I'll do the inventory. Besides, I had time to unwind today playing golf with Regal. It's nothing for me to take thirty minutes to do the inventory when I get home. I know that bakery like the back of my hand."

"Okay, well, I appreciate it."

"You are very welcome, sweet lips."

"How was golf by the way?"

"The norm—I whipped Regal yet again."

Gianna grinned. "Are you on the way home?"

"Not yet. I'm going to swing by Regal's place for a while but I'll be home before you get there. Maybe we can watch a movie and order a pizza and some wings."

"That sounds good—the food and the fact that I'll be curled up next to you," Gianna said.

"And you know I'm always down for some curl-up action with my baby."

When Gianna didn't respond, Ramsey said, "I can see you blushing."

"You can't *see* me doing anything over the

phone, Ramsey."

"So you're *not* blushing right now?"

"Well, I kinda am," she admitted, twirling the necklace he purchased for her. The three-stone diamond.

"I'll see you tonight, baby."

"Okay." Gianna placed her cell phone on the desk, then got up to take the cupcakes she'd forgotten about out of the oven. She certainly wouldn't sell overcooked cupcakes. To her relief, Felicity had already removed them from the oven.

"You're a lifesaver, Felicity," Gianna shouted from the kitchen.

"Love you too, Gianna," Felicity responded.

* * *

Pizza and movie night was more like a make-out session on the sofa. The movie was playing. A pepperoni-sausage-mushroom pizza was on the table, but instead of eating at the moment, Gianna was in her nightshirt stretched out on the sofa while Ramsey was on his knees next to her with his tongue lost somewhere down her throat. She moaned while they kissed and tried to handle him the best way she could but the man was skilled with his mouth the same way he was with architectural designs. Occasionally, he'd let her come up for air, but he was intent on making love to her mouth. The movie could wait.

"Mmm," she said feeling his thick tongue fill her mouth.

Sensing she might need air, he stopped.

Licked her lips.

Licked his.

Licked hers again.

She giggled. "What's wrong with you?"

"What do you mean?"

"You're kissing me like it's your first time...like we haven't done this a trillion times."

"I can't get enough of you." He took another small kiss and said, "Gosh, there are so many things I want to do with you. Show you. We never did get a chance to go whitewater rafting."

"That wasn't because we didn't have time. You know I'm not that adventurous."

"That's why you have me. I'm going to bring the adventure out of you, baby."

"Is that so?"

"Yes. That's so." He combed his fingers through her hair. "I want to travel with you—and I mean take a month away from work and go anywhere in the world we want."

"Anywhere?"

"Yes. Where would you go first, my love?"

"Um, probably California."

Ramsey chuckled. "You can go *anywhere* in the world and you choose California?"

"Yes. I've never been."

"Okay, babe. One day, I'm going to take you to California. Me, you and baby girl."

She smiled. "Me, you and baby girl."

He touched her stomach. "I can't believe you're having my baby. Can't believe how fast things transpired between us."

"I know. I think about it when I'm at the bakery—"

"Oh...you think about me while you're at the bakery whipping up those delicious cupcakes?"

"I do. After all, that is where we met. Where you basically stalked me."

A dimple formed on his cheek. "*I* stalked *you*. Okay."

"I remember the first day you came into the bakery...when you left that day, I honestly didn't expect to see you again. I was shocked when you showed up the next day."

"Surprised me, too. I wasn't expecting a connection. I just wanted some coffee, but when I saw you...I couldn't help myself. And you were funny, too."

"I wasn't being funny on purpose."

"I know. That's what makes you so hilarious...made me even more interested."

"And look at us now."

"Yes. Look at us. Now, you're stuck with me," he said, kissing her stomach.

"I'm not stuck. I *want* to be with you. I enjoy being with you. You're my everything."

Ramsey folded his bottom lip under his teeth. "We need to take this conversation to the bedroom if you're going to talk dirty to me."

Gianna laughed. "That's talking dirty?"

"Yeah. Gianna style."

"Well, if you want to go to the bedroom, you'll get no objections from me."

Ramsey took the remote from the table, powered off the TV and said, "Okay. Let's go.

You walk ahead of me so I can squeeze your booty...get you warmed up."

Gianna giggled. "Stop it. That tickles."

He had a handful of butt-cheek when he responded, "I got something that's gon' tickle you, all right..."

"Ramsey—" Gianna blushed, then gnawed on her bottom lip.

When they stepped into their third-floor master suite, he pulled her into his arms kissing like he was starving for the taste of her while his hands gripped and squeezed her backside even more.

"Mmm," he moaned, just beginning to satisfy his hunger for her. He broke off the kiss to lave her neck with his tongue, feeling her body quiver in his arms. "That tickles, huh?"

"Mmm hmm," she confirmed, still absorbing the feeling, taking it all in.

He pulled up her nightshirt, tugged at her panties until he maneuvered them down the length of her legs, then touched her there – that spot – the one that was sure to make her go insane and stir a fire inside of her.

Gianna threw her head back and closed her eyes. Bit down on her lip.

"Look at me, Gianna."

She opened her eyes to see him – his pit-black, deep, mysterious eyes – staring back at her and he was still stroking her. Teasing her. Driving her wild. Staring into her eyes like he was daring her not to fall apart at his hands. Then, out of nowhere, the most wicked, sexiest smile she'd ever seen came over his face when he asked, "Does that tickle?"

"Ramsey," she gasped with what little oxygen she had at her disposal.

"Huh?" he asked, stroking still, fingers gliding back and forth across her pearl.

"Ramsey..." she sang almost there. He knew she was. He could read her body like the most complicated sketch. It's the only piece of art he'd committed to memory.

He stopped, allowed her to catch her breath, then walks her over to the bed. While they're still standing, he instructed her to place her hands on the mattress.

Gianna could hear the moment his zipper went south. Could hear him wiggling out of jeans and sliding down his boxers and then she felt it – the size of him against her backside, bobbling around before he guided it to home plate. Inch-by-inch he stretched her until her body swallowed him up. Tightened around him. Locked him in. Held him hostage.

All kinds of sensations took over – ones he felt before but would never get used to. He moved back and forth, stroking her back with his fingertips then played with her hair – pacing his tempo according to what he thought she could handle. He listened to her moan, felt her body shake and he knew she was about to come apart.

"Ramsey!" she bellowed, lowering herself from hands to forearms as tremors rattled her body. He leaned down so his chest rested on her back. Holding her steady. She was still standing – legs weak from the pleasure tearing through her – but still standing. Body steady quivering. Moans still filling the room. Triggered by her moans and screams, he let out one of his own, exploding, emptying himself inside of her in a good-to-the-last-drop way, feeling every nerve-ending alive and pouring out pleasure intermittently, sending an electric charge throughout their bedroom – prolonging the intensity of his climax.

And then they rested together, naked and in love, lying on top of the covers fully spent and one-hundred-percent in love.

# Chapter 12

When Monday rolled around, the men of St. Claire Architects – Ramsey, Regal, Royal, Romulus, and the project managers, Ralph and Gilbert – were all in Uptown with Basile Moreau at the future home of some French fashions coming to Charlotte. Standing at five feet, nine inches, Basile was shorter than the St. Claire brothers but he was dressed in a way that made him fit in. Well, somewhat. He had on a dark teal suit, with a camel-colored pair of Bestetti shoes and a pair of ombre sunglasses with lenses that transitioned from black to clear. He was impressed with St. Claire Architect's ability to deliver a prime location within the heart of the city – just what he was looking for. It was one thing to see the site on a map – but it proved to be another experience to actually be there to see the premium Uptown location with his own eyes. The streets were overflowing with people. All Basile saw were dollar signs.

"You've certainly outdone yourself, Ramsey," Basile said in a strong French accent.

"I can't take the credit for this leg of the project." Ramsey patted Romulus on the shoulder. "This is the man who made it happen."

"Romulus, thank you. I'm most grateful," Basile said.

"Just doing my job," Romulus said modestly.

"Basile, what do you say we grab some lunch, then we'll head back to the office to give you a tour and discuss a few more details," Ramsey said.

"Yes. This sounds good to me."

* * *

The men settled in at Palm, and after being served their food, Regal asked, "So, Basile..."

"Yes," he said in the middle of eating a roasted pepper salmon fillet.

"This new building is going to be for some French fashion. Will you carry men's fashion, or will this be another store catered to women?"

"We'll actually do both and it's very high-end clothing, Regal. The minimum price for a suit is five grand."

"Whew," Ralph said. "That's a little steep for my wallet."

"I'm with you on that, Ralph," Gilbert said.

"I'm sure you've priced the Charlotte market," Ramsey said glancing up at Basile. "Are you confident in selling those kinds of suits here in the Queen City? I'll be a customer for sure, but not everyone can afford a suit with that kind of price tag attached."

Basile fanned his napkin open to dab his mouth, then said, "Charlotte is prime for this kind of venture. We looked at New York first and while it was a contender, the fashion scene in New York is a little too eclectic for our taste."

Regal had just taken a gulp of soda. Then he commented, "So you're saying Charlotteans dress better than New Yorkers."

Basile smirked – an uncommon expression for the businessman but leave it up to Regal to get Basile to loosen up a bit. "No, Regal...I assure you that's not what I mean."

"Let me ask you this then," Regal said, on a roll with questions. "Who started the trend of wearing tight, high-water suits with ashy ankles...no socks?"

Amused, Romulus could only shake his head.

Royal glanced up at Regal and kept on eating.

Ramsey was amused himself, but tried to hide it by continuing to eat.

"Please...help me to understand what a *high water* suit is," Basile said.

Royal laughed.

Ramsey cleared his throat and explained, "I think my brother is referring to pants that tapers off at the ankles."

"Oh. I think the American designers came up with that concept. Personally, I prefer full-length suits."

"I agree," Romulus chimed in, "And not the ones that make it hard to move around freely."

"Yeah...gotta have room for the crown jewels," Regal said.

Basile grinned. "That *is* a must."

Ramsey took a sip of green tea and was about to shift the conversation from Regal and *jewels* when he saw a woman who looked like Geraldine breeze pass the front windows of the restaurant. He could have sworn it was her. Only one way to find out.

"Gentlemen, excuse me for a moment," he said getting up, heading for the door. He followed the woman – was almost certain it was Geraldine now. The gold rings on her fingers gave her away. She wore more jewelry than Jezebel.

Ramsey continued following her to see where she was going at two-something in the afternoon on a Monday. Walking with a fierce strut, the heels of her shoes drummed on the sidewalk and as she entered one of the towers. He followed using the rotating doors.

When she disappeared down the hallway, he stayed back so she didn't see him and after waiting for a few beats, he came around the corner but she wasn't there, which meant she was in one of the two offices on this wing – a therapist office or a public accountant office.

She could have been in either, but he took an educated guess and stepped inside the place she'd most needed to visit – the therapist.

He opened the door and sure enough, there she was sitting in a waiting area already flipping through a magazine.

Geraldine looked up and saw him. Her eyes brightened in surprise.

"Ramsey St. Claire...what are you doing here?"

"I was primed and ready to ask you the same thing, Geraldine."

Geraldine tossed the magazine back onto the wicker table and said, "I'm sure Gianna told you she met with me."

Ramsey invited himself to sit down a chair away from her to keep some space between them. "She did."

"And let me guess—you're against it. Here to threaten me and tell me to leave her alone. You make it so obvious that you don't like me."

"That's because I don't trust you, and I know how much my wife had to suffer because of you. I know the pain you've caused her. Am I to believe you're on a path of righting your wrongs and fixing your damaged relationship with Gianna and Gemma?"

"I am. I've seen the errors of my ways," Geraldine said holding her head high trying to salvage her pride, what little she had left, anyway. "And I'm not going to let you stop me."

Ramsey crossed his legs. "Don't make the mistake of thinking Gianna belongs to you, Geraldine. She's mine and always will be. Now, since you're sitting in this therapist office, I suppose I can conclude you're actually making an effort with trying to repair your relationship with my wife."

"I told you I was."

"Then you have to understand me when I tell you I'm protective of what's mine. Gianna is carrying my child. She doesn't need any of the stress and flat-out foolishness you brought to her in the past."

"I understand that."

Ramsey's brows raised. "You do?"

"Yes."

"All right." Ramsey uncrossed his legs and stood up. "Then it's time to show and prove. I want you to join us for dinner on Wednesday evening."

Geraldine looked surprised. "What did you say?"

"I want you to join us for dinner on Wednesday," Ramsey repeated. "In fact, I'll talk to Royal so he can discuss it with Gemma and maybe they can join us as well. Do you know where I live?"

"I do."

"Good. I'll expect to see you there by 7:30 p.m."

"O-okay," Geraldine said, still somewhat shocked about the invite. "I'll be there."

"Are you sure? You don't sound convincing."

"Yes. I'm sure. I'll be there."

"Good. I'll be on my way now," Ramsey said, then walked out the door.

* * *

When he was back to the restaurant, Ramsey pulled Royal off to the side but before he could talk to him about Geraldine, Royal said, "It's not like you to be handling outside business when we're dealing with a priority client. What's so urgent?"

"That's what I was just about to discuss with you. I got up because I saw Geraldine walk by. I caught up with her—asked her to come by the house for dinner on Wednesday."

Royal lifted a brow. "You're kidding."

"I'm not. Geraldine has been attempting to get herself together and I think our wives need to see her effort. They need this in their lives."

"Maybe *your* wife does. Gemma doesn't need the stress and I don't want to subject her to that lunatic, so if that's what you're asking, the answer is heck no."

"Take a day to think it over, Royal. You're basing your decisions on your own emotions. I don't like Geraldine, either, but I'm thinking about how Gianna would feel. That's what I'm asking you to do. Put yourself in Gemma's shoes. Think about Gemma's feelings."

"I *am* thinking about Gemma. I consider my wife in all of my decisions," Royal said sounding slightly offended.

"Then you know she needs this just as much as Gianna does."

"No, she needs a mother—not a maniac who pops in and out of her life, plays with her emotions then goes flying off to the moon on her broom."

Tickled, Ramsey struggled to keep a serious face when he responded, "Think it over. She'll be at the house on Wednesday."

"I assume you've already talked this over with Gianna."

"Not yet, but based on previous conversations we've already had about Geraldine I'm sure she'll be okay with it. We have our first childbirth class tonight. I'll mention it to her then."

"And you're absolutely sure she'll go for it?"

"Yes. Gianna has already expressed a desire to give Geraldine a chance."

Royal nodded. Blew a breath. "All right. I'll think about it. Now, let's go get Regal out of this restaurant. He's been in rare form today. What's with him?"

"Not sure. Maybe he had a good night."

Royal grinned wickedly. "So did I, but I'm not talking about my crown jewels."

The men laughed.

"Yeah, let's get him out of there before Basile starts to think he's a lil' flaky," Ramsey said.

Royal smirked. "It's Regal...of course he's flaky."

"Yeah, but our clients don't need to know that."

"True. Let's go."

# Chapter 13

Gianna sat on a mat, listening while the instructor, an ex-yoga teacher, instructed all the men in the childbirth class to sit behind their wives. Leave it to Ramsey to not only sit behind Gianna but also spread his legs wide while cradling his pelvis right up against her butt. He rested his hands on her stomach while fluttering his tongue at the nape of her neck.

Gianna jerked at the sensation of his hot tongue touching her neck. "Ramsey, stop it. The instructor keeps looking over here."

"Let her look. I don't care."

"I do," she whispered frantically.

"There's no need to be shy, Gianna. Everyone knows what we had to do to get to this point."

Gianna's face turned red.

And to make her blush with hotness even more, Ramsey whispered in her ear, "They know I was inside of you, baby. If they knew how many times..." he whistled. "You wouldn't be trying to act so innocently right now."

A flush crept across her face. Gianna smiled, drowning in his heat. His scent. The powerful man that he was. He was so serious about work. Dedicated to it, she knew, but not as much as he was dedicated to her and their baby. He never lost his craving for her since the beginning of their courtship and marriage, and she would never get used to the way he made her feel. Wanted. Desired.

"Okay fathers," the instructor said. "I want you to hold your spouse's hand and practice some deep breathing."

The corner of his mouth lifted. "From what I saw last night, you got this deep breathing stuff down already," Ramsey said, taking Gianna's hand into his.

"Yes, I do."

"Okay," the instructor said, "You're going to take a deep breath through your nose and release it slowly out of your mouth. So, breathe in…"

Gianna pulled in a long breath then released it slowly. She repeated this while Ramsey closed his eyes, left little kisses beside her face, then kept his face pressed against hers. "I have to talk to you about something."

"Right now?" she asked, then pulled in a deep breath, releasing slowly again following directions.

"Yes."

"Ramsey, you're supposed to be helping me with these relaxation techniques."

"I am, baby, but this can't wait."

"Okay," she said, "But when I go into labor and snatch your lips off of your face because I don't know how else to deal with the pain, it's your own fault."

Ramsey chuckled. "You're not going to be

that bad. I know for a fact you can handle a little pain."

She narrowed her eyes at him.

"Sorry, I couldn't resist that one."

"What do you want to talk about?"

"I saw Geraldine today."

"Where?"

"In Uptown. You know I had that meeting with the French designer—"

"Un huh."

"While we were eating lunch, I saw Geraldine walk by, so I got up and followed her."

Gianna's eyes grew big. "You followed her?"

"I did. I wanted to see where she was going, especially since you said she told you she was ready to make a change and whatnot."

"And?" Gianna said, following the instructor's directions by extending her arm straight up into the air. "Where was she going?"

Ramsey ran his hands up her arm's length and back down again. "She went to see a therapist."

"She did?" Gianna asked feeling a sense of relief. Geraldine had told her she wanted to make a change and, according to Ramsey, she was seeing a therapist. That was not only a step in the right direction for her but also the proof Gianna needed that Geraldine was serious this time.

"Yes. I followed her into the office and had a talk with her."

"Are you serious, Ramsey? I can't believe you actually followed her. And what do you mean you had a *talk* with her? You hate Geraldine with a passion."

"I don't hate her. I just don't *like* her. Anyway, after my chat with her, I realized something."

"What's that?"

"That I owe you an apology."

Gianna put her arms down and gave Ramsey her attention. "Why?"

"You were interested in trying to establish some kind of relationship with Geraldine and I wasn't being supportive. I should've been, but I wasn't. I was being more protective than actually listening to you, and that's why I'm apologizing—for not listening when you needed me to. I'm sorry."

"I appreciate that, Ramsey. Now, tell me how this *talk* went."

"It was progress for me because I still don't necessarily trust your mother, but she does appear to be making an effort, so I invited her over for dinner."

"You did what!" Gianna yelled so loud the entire class stopped and looked at her. "Oops. Sorry."

Ramsey buried his face in her neck and laughed.

"Stop laughing at me, Ramsey."

"You are something else. Why do you react so strongly to things?"

"I'm—I'm in shock...can't believe you invited her to dinner."

"Well, I did."

"To our home?"

"Yes."

"What do you think about it?"

"I think that's a *huge* step for you but I also believe it will help me and Gemma."

"That's what I was thinking. Royal wasn't too fond of having Gem anywhere near Geraldine, so if you think it's a good idea, you may want to talk to her or possibly him about it."

"I'll call Royal when we get home."

"So, it's settled? You're okay with Geraldine coming over?" Ramsey asked as his fingers wiggled up her maternity blouse.

Gianna squirmed and giggled, her body quivering at his touch. "Ye-yes. I'm fine with it. Now stop."

"I don't want to stop," he said, and he didn't.

"Ramsey," Gianna said, giggling. "The teacher is going to kick us out."

"Okay, okay," he said, "But you gon' get it later."

\* \* \*

Gianna was sitting on the sofa, getting hungrier by the second at the smell of whatever it was Carson was preparing for dinner. Ramsey was in his office checking for an email he needed to respond to according to an urgent text from Judy. He would've replied using his phone, but he found it easier to do so on his laptop in his office where he could concentrate.

In the interim, Gianna took the opportunity to call Royal, thinking it was appropriate to talk with him first before taking the issue straight to Gemma. If Royal told Ramsey he didn't like the idea of Gemma being at dinner with Geraldine, chances are he probably didn't mention anything about the dinner to her just yet. She reached for the remote to turn the volume down on the TV and dialed Royal's number.

"What up, G?" he answered.

Gianna was smiling when she said, "Hey, Royal."

"Hey...surprised to see you calling me. What has Ramsey done? Do you need me to handle him for you?"

"No," Gianna said, all smiles.

"I'm just kidding. You got Ramsey under your thumb. If you're looking for Gemma, she's taking a shower at the moment while I'm preparing dinner."

"*You're* cooking dinner?"

"I am—making nachos—got the kitchen smelling heavenly over here."

"That's cool. I know Gemma appreciates having a live-in chef."

A chuckle escaped. "She does."

Gianna smiled. "Um...anyway, I called to talk to you about something."

"To me?"

"Yes, about Geraldine. Ramsey said he mentioned dinner—"

"He did," Royal cut in to say, "And I'll admit I didn't like the idea one bit."

"Why not?"

"Do you really have to ask me that, Gianna? You know, just as well as I do, that your mother ain't working with a full deck. Need I remind you of the hospital incident?"

"No. Ramsey already has, but he's come around since then."

"And so have you, I take it."

"Well, I—um—look…I think Geraldine is trying, and since that's the case, we need to try, too."

Royal sighed audibly. Heavily.

"I know how much you love Gemma."

"I don't think you do. You know what you *see*, Gianna, but you can't begin to fathom the depths of which I love your sister. I know you love her, too, but it's my job to protect her and look out for her now. With that in mind, do you think I want Gemma to meet up with Geraldine?"

"No," Gianna said downcast. "But it'll be at our house in a comfortable setting. Ramsey won't allow any discord in the house and he definitely won't let Geraldine go off on a tirade—not saying I think that's what she'll do—I'm just saying. Everything will be fine, and if at any point Gemma wants to leave, she can."

"All right. I'll do it for you, but you remember this the next time you bake some blueberry lemon cupcakes."

Gianna giggled. The blueberry flavors were among Royal's favorites. "Okay. I will."

"And thank you for coming directly to me concerning this. You could've gone straight to Gem."

"Could have, but I didn't want to usurp your

authority. I've spent a long time taking care of and guarding my sister. Now, that responsibility falls on you."

"And I gladly accept."

Gianna smiled.

"When is this dinner with broom-rider, I mean, Geraldine?"

Gianna chuckled. "Wednesday, say around 7:30."

"Got it. We'll be there. I'll talk it over with Gemma tonight."

"Thanks, Royal. I owe you one."

"Nah...you *owe* me some blueberry cupcakes."

Tickled, Gianna responded, "I'll have your cupcake payment ready. No worries."

He chuckled. "Okay, Gianna. We'll see you on Wednesday."

"Okay. Enjoy your nachos and tell Gem I said, hi."

"Will do. See ya."

"Bye."

# Chapter 14

Ramsey left his office around 9:50 a.m. and arrived at the bakery around 10:05 a.m. where he sat and sipped coffee while Gianna was in the kitchen working. The first interviewee was scheduled to arrive at 10:15, and while he waited, he reviewed Beth's resume again. Seemed she had worked at a bakery before but had noted on her resume that the place had closed down.

The doorbell chimed. Ramsey twisted his body to look behind him and that's when he saw the Caucasian woman standing there clutching her purse. A brunette. She looked nervous. Mid-forties. A little stocky for her height.

"Good morning," he greeted her.

"Good morning."

Ramsey stood up, walked over to her and said, "You must be Beth."

"I am...here for the interview."

He reached to shake her hand. "Right. I'm Ramsey St. Claire."

"Nice to meet you, Mr. St. Claire. Are you the owner?"

"No. My wife runs this place. Have a seat, get comfortable and I'll see if I can pry her out of the kitchen."

"All right," the woman said, setting her purse on the table next to the table where Ramsey was originally sitting.

Ramsey walked to the back, saw Gianna frosting cupcakes. "Gianna, baby," he said putting his arms around her, resting his hands on her stomach. "It's time for the first interview."

"Shoot. Okay, let me frost these last five and I'll be right out."

"Take your time," he told her, then walked back to the front and asked Beth, "Hey, can I get you some coffee, water or milk? It's on the house."

"Coffee would be nice."

Ramsey took a large cup and filled it with coffee. He placed it on the table. "Not sure how you take yours but there's cream and sugar over there."

"This is fine, actually."

Gianna came from the back, still wearing her apron and hairnet. "Hey, sorry about that."

"No worries," Ramsey said, "Beth, this is my wife Gianna. Gianna, Beth."

Gianna's eyes grew big when the woman turned around. "Beth?"

"Oh my word...Gianna Jacobsen?" Beth said, astounded.

"My gosh, it's so good to see you!" Gianna said, giving her a hug.

Ramsey smiled as he watched on. Apparently, the women knew each other.

"Ramsey, this is Beth Woodley—the woman who taught me how to make cupcakes at the bakery I used to work at after I graduated high school."

"It's been a long time," Beth said.

"Yes, it has," Gianna agreed, beside herself with excitement.

"And you're married now."

"Yes, with a little one on the way," Gianna said, touching her stomach.

"Congratulations!"

"Thank you. I'm excited. Oh, and you already met my husband, Ramsey."

"Yes," Beth said. "So, it's not Gianna Jacobson anymore."

"No. It's St. Claire now," Gianna told her. "Are you interested in the position?"

"I am. You heard what happened to Street Sweets, right?" Street Sweets was the name of the bakery where Beth and Gianna used to work together.

"Last I heard they had moved to Plaza Midwood, hoping to get more business," Gianna said.

Ramsey sat down, crossed his legs and watched the women converse.

"Well, the owner, Marge—you remember Marge don't you?"

"Yes."

"She died. Her husband tried to keep the place up and running in her honor, you know, but poor Tanner—he was so heartbroken...didn't make it three months. He couldn't run the place without her. Had to shut it down."

"That's so sad. Was Marge sick?"

"Something like that. They were tight-lipped about her health issues with the staff, but when she stopped working, we all knew that wasn't a good sign. You know how much Marge loved baking."

Gianna nodded. "I remember. Yes. And what about Tanner? How's he?"

"He moved to Virginia to be with his family. I'm sure that'll be good for him."

"Yes. No doubt." Gianna glanced at Ramsey, noticing him sipping coffee while flipping through his phone. "Oh, I'm sorry Ramsey. We're just over here playing catch-up and you're waiting to do the interview."

"Take your time. I'm in no hurry," Ramsey said, setting his phone off to the side giving her his attention. "Since you two know each other, do you think an interview is necessary?"

"Not really," Gianna said. "Beth literally taught me the basics of baking. I don't think I would have succeeded in this business without her."

"Is it safe to say we don't need to do anymore interviewing?" Ramsey asked Gianna.

"I would say so. Beth, if you want the job—"

"Yes, I want the job!"

"Awesome. Are you familiar with the hours?"

"No."

"Well, we're closed on Sunday and Monday. Tuesday through Friday, we open at 10:30 a.m. and close at 7:00 p.m. I usually get here in the mornings before ten to get a jump start on the morning rush."

"That will fit perfectly into my schedule."

"Good. Um...am I forgetting anything, Ramsey?" Gianna asked him.

"Just the application." He opened a folder and removed one. "We'll need an official application on file. Also, we will conduct a background check. Other than that..." He thought a moment and said, "Oh...the wages were listed in the ad, correct?"

"Yes, and I'm fine with twenty dollars an hour."

"Great, then we hope to have you on board within the next two weeks," Ramsey said.

"Awesome," Beth said.

"Then it's settled," Gianna told her. "I'll be in touch."

"We definitely need to catch up."

"Yes, we do and we will. It's so good to see you." Gianna hugged her.

"You too. And it was nice to meet you as well," she said to Ramsey.

"Likewise. Please return the application as soon as you can."

"I'll have it back to you by tomorrow," Beth said. "Should I just drop it off here?"

"Yes. I'll be here," Gianna told her.

"Okay, well enjoy the rest of your day and thank you so much for the opportunity."

"You're welcome, Beth," Gianna said.

Beth made her way to the door. After she was gone, Ramsey looked at Gianna and said, "That worked out."

"It did. Wow! I had no idea she was one of the applicants. It's almost like it was meant to be."

"Just like us," Ramsey said circling his arms around her. "I'll have Judy notify the other candidates that the position is filled unless you want to wait until Beth's background check comes back."

"We don't have to wait. I know Beth. She'll pass with flying colors."

"Then it's settled."

"Yes, it's settled. Once again you've come to my rescue," she said gazing into Ramsey's eyes.

"Ramsey St. Claire, at your service, baby," he said before lowering his mouth to hers taking a long kiss until the sweet taste of her soaked into his taste buds. When it hit him, he absorbed it. Savored it. Enjoyed the feel of her tongue in his mouth. He moaned as he broke the kiss, not wanting to do it, but he knew she had to get back to work, and so did he. "I'll be at the office for the rest of the day if you need me."

"Okay."

"And don't forget Geraldine's coming over for dinner this evening."

"How could I possibly forget that?"

Ramsey chuckled. "If the woman starts acting crazy, I'm kicking her out."

"As you should," Gianna said. "But I have a feeling that this time will be different."

"Let's hope so for her sake."

# Chapter 15

Dinner started off tense. For one, Geraldine showed up thirty minutes late and Gianna and Gemma had grown increasingly doubtful with the passing of every minute she was late, thinking that, once again, Geraldine had lied to them. So, when she finally showed up at a few minutes before eight, they hid frustration behind fake smiles and small talk not knowing exactly how to begin *the* conversation they desperately needed to have.

That's when Royal had heard enough. Small talk didn't count for much to him. They needed *big* talk that would answer some tough questions so he decided to end the shenanigans by asking, "Geraldine, what made you want to do this now after you've wasted so many years?"

Geraldine frowned slightly when she glanced up at Royal, but he didn't back down. Wasn't in his nature to. He held her gaze – eyes dared her to act out of pocket, but she stayed quiet. She was either irritated or thinking of a clever way to answer his question.

Ramsey smirked, watching this silent battle of see-who-blinks-first. It definitely wouldn't be Royal. And here he was thinking it was him who'd crank up the heat on Geraldine...

Royal beat him to the punch.

"Well, I won't sit here and run down excuses as to why I did this or that."

Royal's face went slack. "You don't think your daughters need to know?"

"They *already* know," she answered. "I was selfish. I wasn't ready for children—I wasn't in the right frame of mind to have children."

"But you did," Royal said, "And while I appreciate your *effort* in coming here to sit down and talk with us, it's going to take more than a couple of hours over a dinner, which you arrived thirty minutes late, to fix the extensive damage you've caused over the years."

Geraldine nodded, feeling defeated. She'd gotten the third degree from Ramsey. Now, she was getting it from Royal. She felt like her efforts were in vain but she knew if she wanted a relationship with her daughters again, she couldn't give up now.

All eyes were locked in on her as everyone waited to see how she would respond. Would she go off on a tangent, flailing her gold ring-draped fingers in everyone's face while telling them how they should respect her because she was their mother and she gave birth to them? Would she cross her legs and just sit there pouting?

They got their answer when she responded, "You're absolutely right. I can't argue against that. All I know is, I messed up and I have to start somewhere to begin repairing the damage I've caused. My behavior in the past—the hospital incident, the lunch we had, Gemma—even down to me not telling you girls about your fathers. I'm sorry I wasn't there for you two when you were growing up. I'm sorry our relationship isn't what it should be but I promise if you give me a chance, it'll be different this time."

Royal leaned back in his chair. He was not a believer. She sounded like a broken record – like an abusive man who put his wife in the hospital for the third time, then came toting her a bouquet of flowers and promising that *it would never happen again* when everyone else knew it would except for the battered wife. So, no, he didn't believe her. Didn't trust her and he wasn't sure he would ever get to that point.

"I'm holding you to that, Geraldine," Ramsey said. "I'm sure you can tell that we—Royal and myself—are very much in love with your daughters. Gianna is my heart and I don't want anything to happen to her. It hurts me to see her sad—it's my job to protect her, her heart, our baby and anyone Gianna loves, which includes Gemma. So I'm going to allow this to happen, but the minute I get the *slightest* hint that something's awry, I'm pulling the plug. Understood?

"Yes, I understand."

"Good." Ramsey stood up. "Royal take a walk with me so we can give the women some privacy."

Royal grimaced, still not trusting Geraldine enough to leave Gemma alone with her. He didn't care that Gianna was present for extra backup. Something just didn't feel right.

"Royal," Ramsey said to get his attention, already reading his thoughts.

"Will you be okay if I step out for a minute, Gemma?" Royal asked her.

"Yes. I'll be fine." Gemma grabbed his shirt, drew him to her and kissed his lips, then whispered, "Don't worry. I'll be fine," for added reassurance.

"Okay," he said, finally leaving the room, following Ramsey outside onto the patio.

Royal inhaled deep breaths of the night air then asked, "Do you think she's serious?"

"I want to believe so, but at this point, she has to show us she's serious. I *will* say she's different from the Geraldine I met at the hospital."

Royal nodded. He could see that as well, but all he could focus on was Gemma. Her feelings on the matter are all he really cared about. He couldn't have this lady in and out of her life, messing things up for her. Toying with her emotions.

"It's crazy being in love and actually being able to feel what your spouse is feeling. I've never experienced anything like it until now. When Gemma's happy, I'm happy. When she's hurting, I'm hurting."

Ramsey cracked a smile. "That's how it's supposed to be. That's how you know you're truly in love." He sat down kicked up his feet on another patio chair and said, "We'll let it play out. I hope it works out for the best for our wives' sake."

"Yep," Royal said.

"How is Gemma doing otherwise?"

"She's good. She's making progress on the foundation, taking an online class and working part-time. I'm proud of her."

"What about the medication? Does the doctor think she needs more chemo?"

"No. The surgery pretty much eliminated the need for chemo. And as for the pills, some days they make her queasy. Those are usually the days she's more exhausted. Other days, she can handle them better and she's more energetic." Royal smiled. "She's a fighter, that's for sure. She gives me motivation to get off my butt and make things happen."

"So, that's why you've been coming to work on time lately," Ramsey quipped. "I'll have to thank Gemma before she leaves tonight."

Royal laughed.

"That's good, though. It's a win-win when your better half makes you better. Gianna certainly makes me better."

"Yeah. The chatter around the office is, you're easier to get along with. I don't see employees speed-walking down the hallway chanting, 'Ramsey's on a rampage... *Ramsey's on a rampage'!*" Royal laughed.

"I *will* be on a rampage if this grass situation at the new University City site isn't fixed soon. Has Ralph said anything to you about it yet?"

"This is the first I'm hearing about it. What's up?" Royal asked while looking through the window to see the women still talking. All was well, so he took a seat.

"I met Ralph at the site last Thursday—he wanted me to check out the landscaping. As soon as I pulled up, I see brown grass."

Royal knew how meticulous his brother was about the business – about everything, really – so he didn't question him as to why brown grass was a big deal. If Ramsey didn't like it, somebody had better get it fixed. "I'll get with Ralph and take care of it."

"Don't do anything yet. Ralph's a project manager. He should be able to handle this. I told him to let you know if he ran into a roadblock. Since you haven't heard anything, I take it he's handling it. At least, I *hope* he's handling it."

"If he runs into a problem, do you want me to take care of it, or—?"

"No. I think I'll handle this one. Hopefully, it won't come to that, but if it does, CitySites will feel my wrath."

Royal chuckled. He stretched out his legs, extended his arms in the air. "How's Gianna doing?"

"Good. The pregnancy hasn't been that rough on her. Baby's growing fine. Oh, and we think we have found a new assistant for the bakery—a woman Gianna used to work with."

"That's good, Ram."

"Yeah, Gianna was excited about it, although, I can tell she doesn't want to stop working."

"Dang. You married your twin," Royal joked.

Ramsey chuckled. "I got a hunch that when the baby comes, she'll forget all about work."

"Are you planning on taking some time off?"

"At least the first six months. I'll be available part-time from home but I won't let work get in the way of bonding with my daughter."

Royal nodded.

"It's funny...sometimes I go stand out on the balcony and daydream about them—Gianna and the baby—thinking about when our daughter is old enough to recognize us. Then when she's a toddler, she'll be running around the bakery and the house, tearing things up, being bossy like me and sweet like her mother."

"Yeah. That's cool, man. Gemma's already agreed that we'll watch her anytime you and Gianna need a date night. I know you ain't adding babysitting to Carson's agenda."

"No. Carson has enough on his plate, although the old man hinted he'd be 'grandpa Carson' to her." Ramsey lowered his feet from the chair to the deck.

"Ay, dinner's coming up this Sunday at mom and dad's," Royal said.

"I know. Mother called me at the office and nearly threatened my life if I didn't show up, like I *wouldn't* show up. I always show up."

"Nah, there was that one time you missed."

"*One* time."

Royal laughed. "If it makes you feel any better, mom called me, too—no threats, though."

"You're lucky."

Royal glanced through the window again, saw Gemma, Gianna and Geraldine laughing. Looked like the conversation was going well.

"It'll be good for everybody to get together. It seems like we've been going our own separate ways lately. Outside of the office, I have no clue what Romulus and Regal are up to these days."

"Oh, that's easy," Ramsey said. "Regal ain't up to nothing and Romulus—" Ramsey shook his head thinking about how much Romulus loved Siderra but seemed blind to that fact. "Let's just say he's in for the ride of his life and doesn't even know it."

"Everybody sees that coming," Royal said.

"Yeah, everybody except him, apparently."

"Siderra ain't going to wait around forever," Royal said. "He'll find out soon enough."

"Let's hope it's sooner rather than later."

Royal stood up. Stretched. "Okay...gotta check on my sweetheart. I think we're going to get going...gotta make sure she's good and relaxed before she goes to sleep."

"In other words, you trying to slip out early so you can *put her to bed*."

"You know it. She 'bout to get a dose of melatonin and I ain't talking about the pill."

Ramsey laughed, stood up and slapped hands with his brother. "You're a fool, man."

"Ay, she already knows what's up, with her pretty, lil' self." Royal nibbled on his lip.

"All right, man, well you go handle that."

"Oh, I intend to."

Ramsey followed Royal inside.

"How's everything in here?" Ramsey asked once they reached the dining room.

"It's okay," Gianna said. "I think we were just wrapping up."

"Good," Royal said. "Because we're going to get going. Gemma's got a long night ahead of her."

Gemma looked at Royal, surprised. "I do?" she questioned.

"Yeah, you do," Royal said firmly, then slowly licked his lips.

"Oh, yes. I do," Gemma said, giddy, quickly getting up from her seat. "Bye, y'all. We'll talk again soon, Geraldine."

Gianna laughed at her sister.

"Bye, Gemma," Geraldine said, standing. "I guess I better be heading out, too." She left right behind Royal and Gemma.

Ramsey and Gianna stood on the steps watching cars pull out of the driveway. "How did it go?"

"It went okay. Geraldine did a lot of talking...explained a lot to Gemma, most of which she'd already told me. I think it helped Gemma a lot. I'm glad we did this. Thank you, Ramsey."

"You're welcome, sweetie. Now, come on. I know you're tired."

"I am. I'm so ready for bed."

"Then let's get ready for bed," Ramsey said, taking her hand in his, leading her back inside of the house.

# Chapter 16

"I brought your blueberry lemon cupcakes, Royal," Gianna said after she greeted everyone. She and Ramsey were the last to arrive for Sunday dinner.

"You didn't have to do that," Royal said.

"Yes you did, Gianna," Gemma chimed in. "Royal is addicted. Do you hear me? A-ddicted. No lie."

Royal chuckled along with Gianna, then he whispered in Gemma's ear, "Stop telling my secrets."

She snuck a quick kiss from his lips since he was so close.

"Hopefully this will be enough to tide you over for a while," Gianna told him.

"It will. I appreciate it," he replied.

"No problem."

"I feel some kind of way about my woman baking another man his own personal cupcakes," Ramsey said.

"Stop that mess, Ramsey," Bernadette said tickled.

"I'm serious." Ramsey pulled out a chair for Gianna at the dinner table.

"He's not serious," Gianna said, sitting down, getting comfortable. "Ramsey knows I'll bake all kinds of cupcakes for him."

"You need to bake a big one with yourself inside of it—that's what he really wants," Regal said. "A Gianna cake."

"Oh, you better believe I already have one of those," Ramsey said, then leaned forward to kiss her.

"Oh, that's *too* much information," Romulus said.

"I was thinking the same thing, Romulus," Bernadette told him.

Gianna sat there with blushed cheeks.

"I wanna know what Royal did to deserve a dozen cupcakes?" Regal asked Gianna. "You ain't never baked no cupcakes for me."

"You've had some of my cupcakes before, Regal."

"Yeah, but not my *own* personal batch. I'm all alone in that big house with no one to do anything for me."

"That's not true," Bernadette said. "You have Primrose."

"Primrose doesn't cook. She just keeps the house clean and tidy. I need a woman that can get up in the kitchen and straight get it stanky."

Mason chuckled. "I heard that."

"See, Dad knows where I'm coming from."

"Of course. Your mother has been stanking up our kitchen for years."

The family chuckled.

"That's what I'm talking about," Regal said. "When you sprinkle *love* on food, it tastes so much better. I need somebody at my crib to sprinkle some *love*."

"Oh, hush that mess, Regal." Bernadette chuckled. "You don't want love." She placed a basket of Hawaiian rolls on the table.

"Of course I want love. Everyone wants love."

"Then why have you never been serious with a woman?" she asked. "Your mama ain't blind. You've had prospects."

The brothers stayed silent during the conversation, but all eyes focused on Regal to see how he would respond.

He shrugged casually. "I haven't found the right one yet. That's all, Mama."

"Whatever you say, Regal." Bernadette moved on with tasks as she glanced up at Romulus. "How are you this evening, Romulus?"

Romulus looked up from his phone. He'd just sent Siderra a text, trying to figure out where she was. He'd called her on the drive but didn't get an answer. "I'm good, Ma."

"Ay, Rom, where's your BFF?" Regal asked Romulus. By 'BFF', everyone knew he was referring to Siderra. She frequented their family dinners like she was a part of the family. She and Romulus had been best friends for so long, she was like family.

Romulus opened his mouth to answer when Bernadette spoke up and said, "Oh, Siderra isn't going to make it tonight."

Romulus appeared confused when he asked, "How do you know that? She called you?"

"She did."

"Did she say why she couldn't come?" he

asked.

"Yes, something about a date."

Romulus frowned. "A date?"

"That's what she said."

The frown remained on his forehead when he asked further, "With who?"

"I don't know. I didn't pry, son. I just told her to have a good time."

Ramsey looked at Romulus seeing the distress on his face. Royal and Regal saw it, too.

"I'm surprised she didn't tell *you*, Romulus," Regal said, "Being that y'all are usually joined at the hip."

"Well, looks like she's going to be attached to someone else's hip tonight," Mason said.

Regal erupted in laughter. "Good one, Dad."

Bernadette nudged her husband for being so crude.

Romulus' frown ditched deeper. He stood up with his cell phone in his hand and said, "I'll be right back."

Bernadette shook her head wordlessly. Siderra was on a date. What would make him think she would answer the phone right now?

* * *

After dinner and dessert, Bernadette asked Gianna to the living room to talk about the baby shower. "Have you thought about a date yet?" Bernadette inquired after they got comfortable.

"No, but I think it better be sooner than later. I'll be eight months before you know it."

"Ain't that the truth," Bernadette said. "I'm too excited. My first grandchild—I never thought I'd see this day with these picky sons of mine."

Gianna smiled, glancing back into the dining room where she could see the family still sitting around the table. She saw Gemma's head resting on Royal's shoulder. Romulus was sitting there looking lonely without Siderra. Regal was animated as usual and joking with his dad about something and then there was Ramsey – he was sitting in the dining room with the family but his eyes were locked on her so precisely, he may as well had been in the living room with her and Bernadette.

Gianna broke away from his stare to focus on Bernadette. "So you never thought you'd get grandbabies, huh?"

"No. I couldn't see any of my boys getting married. Then, Ramsey got engaged to Leandra but when she died, I just knew that was it for him. Then he found you."

Gianna smiled. "Yeah. Then he found me."

"Praise the Lord for that."

"Do you think it was destined to be?"

"You mean, you and Ramsey?"

"Yes. Sometimes, when I'm alone at the bakery, I sit in my office and think about how screwed up my life would be without him. He's rescued me in so many ways. Before Ramsey, I was a mess."

"He was too, honey, so I think you two are pretty even. But in answer to your question, I do think it was meant to be. I certainly don't believe any other woman could capture his heart the way you have. We've been sitting in here talking, and he hasn't stopped staring at you."

Gianna glanced back at Ramsey and saw him smiling.

"Okay, let's talk about this baby shower—what do you say we do it two weeks from now on a Saturday," Bernadette suggested.

"Um...let me think," Gianna said because the bakery was usually open on Saturdays, but if Beth was working by then, she could run the bakery in her absence. Only problem was, she didn't know exactly when Beth was starting yet, so she responded, "How about two weeks from now on a Sunday. The bakery is open on Saturdays."

"Oh, that's right. Sunday will be fine, then."

"And by the way, Felicity wants to help with planning. Gemma may want to help as well."

"Honey, I could certainly use the help."

Gianna sipped water.

"How are you feeling about becoming a new mother?"

"I'm nervous. I'm excited, too, but more nervous about taking care of a baby. I want to be so much for her—to give her a good life so she doesn't grow up like I did."

"That's understandable. Have you heard from your mother lately?"

"I have. She was at the house this past Wednesday—says she's sorry and wants a relationship with me and Gemma now."

"Do you believe her?"

"I want to, but I think my strong *want* for her to change is the reason I feel like I'm tricking myself into believing things will be different this time."

"I wouldn't worry too much about it, Gianna. Your mother is an adult. You can't be too caught up about whether she's sincere or not. Trust me, if she's not, her true colors will begin to show real soon."

"You're right about that."

"And you already know Ramsey ain't going to tolerate no nonsense out of her."

"He's already stated that to me *and* her."

Bernadette chuckled. "That's what I thought." She glanced up to see Ramsey still staring in their direction. "He's going to be protective of the baby."

"I know," Gianna said, smiling. "Ramsey is such a strong man, yet he's already shown me how compassionate he can be. He's going to be a great father."

"Yes, he is."

"He's already a great husband. I couldn't—" Gianna's voice trailed off as wetness came to her eyes. "I couldn't ask for a better man."

"Aw," Bernadette said, walking towards the powder room and came back with a box of Kleenex. She handed Gianna one and at the same time watched Ramsey get up from the dining room table and head in their direction.

"What's going on in here?" he asked, sitting next to Gianna. "You're crying." He wrapped his arms around her.

"I'm fine, Ramsey," Gianna said, dabbing

her eyes.

"Then why are you crying?" he asked.

"It's probably just the hormones."

"Gianna," he said prompting her to look at him. Her tears were gone, but a mist of wetness remained in her eyes. "Why are you crying?"

"I was just telling your mother how much I love you and I got emotional."

Ramsey glanced at his mother, then back at Gianna when he took her hand, kissed the backside of it and said, "I love you, too, Gianna." He couldn't do what he wanted to do to her – not with his mother sitting there looking at them, so a kiss had to do for now. Then he looked at Bernadette and said, "Ma, you got my wife in here crying?"

"Don't you start with me Ramsey St. Claire," Bernadette said tickled. "*You* got your wife in here crying. She loves you."

Ramsey was all smiles. "I know." He squeezed Gianna's hand. "Did you come up with a date for the baby shower?"

"Yes," Gianna said. "In two weeks. Sunday."

"Cool."

"I'm going to do electronic invitations," Bernadette said. "They'll go out within the next couple of days so if there are people you want to add, let me know Gianna."

"I will."

"Good," Ramsey said. "Sounds like you two have made some progress which is great because I'm taking my baby home now, Mother." Ramsey stood up, extended his hand to Gianna and helped her stand up from the sofa.

"Goodnight, you two. I'll be in touch, Gianna."

# Chapter 17

Ramsey stood at the vanity half naked, wearing only a towel around his bottom half. He'd just showered, brushed his teeth, his hair and used a moisturizer on his skin – his typical nighttime routine – when he saw Gianna walk in wearing a thin, see-through spearmint green gown. She looked like a goddess with her hair loose. Instantly, a smile came to his face. Heat and warmth spread to his heart when she stood behind him and wrapped her arms around his torso.

"I love you," she said.

"I love you, too."

He felt the moment she smiled against his back. Silence lingered in the room while she held him, but he could hear all the things she didn't say, like how much she loved him. Needed him. Admired and respected him. How much she trusted him to be her man. Her other half. Her support. Her leader. Her everything.

"Gianna?"

"Yes," she said softly.

Her warm breath against his back made his

skin crawl. "Are you tired?"

"A little, and just so you know, that'll probably be my answer to that question 'til the baby comes."

Ramsey turned around and took her hands in his. "I know. Whatever I can do to help you, you know I will. As a matter of fact, come here." He led her from the bathroom into the bedroom where he told her to take off her gown. Then, standing in front of her, he removed his towel.

Gianna's eyes grew big when she glanced down at his mid-section and said, "Goodness, gracious. Down boy."

He chuckled and looked down at himself. "What?"

"You want me."

"I always want you. I told you that." He walked over to the closet, came back in a pair of Versace boxers and said, "But not tonight. Tonight, I'm going to massage your feet, your hands, your thighs, that soft butt of yours and anything else that needs your man's attention. Are you good with that, cupcake?"

"Yes."

Ramsey instructed her to lie down on her back while he filled his hands with lotion. He lowered himself to his knees, took one foot in his hand and massaged from toes to heel, applying pressure along the way. Her moans told him she was enjoying it, so he continued on to the other foot, applying pressure, circling his thumb in the arc of her foot causing her to gasp his name.

Inch by inch, he took his time working his way up her legs, rolling his thumbs around her kneecaps and grabbing a firm hold to squeeze her thighs. And he squeezed and massaged them all the way up to the pleasure between her legs. He was tempted, boy was he tempted to massage her there, to make her body quiver uncontrollably but since she was already tired, he bypassed her sweet spot and began massaging her hands – one at a time. Then came her arms, shoulders and before he could get to her back, she'd already fallen asleep.

His eyes traveled the length of her body. He smiled. Then he hugged her belly. With his face against her stomach, he could feel the baby's kicks. "I see somebody's awake," he said. More kicks came. "Hi, baby girl. It's daddy." He placed his hand flat on Gianna's stomach. "I can't wait to meet you. I know you're going to be a sweet, little girl just like your mommy. Before you know it, she'll have you baking cupcakes and acting all quirky just like her. You'll be smart like her, well and me, but your mother will probably be your biggest influencer. I've never met a more driven, determined woman. You're going to learn so much from her, baby girl. I'm proud I chose her to be your mom."

Ramsey kissed Gianna's stomach tenderly, then pulled up the covers after he got comfortable beside her. "Goodnight, Gianna," he whispered since she was already sleeping. He kissed her softly on the cheek, then closed his eyes, resting beside her.

# Chapter 18

Due to an off-site meeting, Ralph missed the morning status meeting so Ramsey made it a point to follow up with him via email regarding the grass issue at the University Complex.

**To**: Ralph Sheppard
**From**: Ramsey St. Claire
**Subject**: Grass @ University City Complex

Ralph,

What's the latest on this issue? Did you receive any pushback from CitySites? Advise at your earliest.

-
RSC

_____

It was around 10:45 a.m. when Ralph responded back:

**To**: Ramsey St. Claire
**From**: Ralph Sheppard

**Subject**: Re: Grass @ University City Complex

I'll come by your office when I get there. They say they are not willing to re-do the grounds there. Said they used premium grass and not responsible for what the elements do to the grass.

-Sent from my mobile device

Ralph Sheppard | Project Manager
St. Claire Architects

————————

Ramsey immediately got on the phone, requesting to speak to Craig Perry, owner of CitySites – a man he'd been working with for years. He wondered if Ralph had spoken with Craig directly or one of the company's project managers.

"Hey, Ramsey. What can I do for you, Sir?"

"I have an issue with one of the sites your team worked—the new apartment complex on University City Boulevard, you know, over there by Ikea."

"Oh, that...ah...yeah...I spoke to your project manager already. I think it was Ralph who called."

"So it was *you* who told Ralph there wasn't an issue."

"I didn't necessarily tell him there was no issue. I told him we're not responsible for the elements and—"

"You're kidding me, right?"

"Unfortunately, I'm not. There's no way I can re-sod that site for free, Ramsey."

"Are you sure about that because I paid you $25,000 and all I got was some pretty flowers and brown grass? There's no way that's premium grass. Premium stays green all year round – hence the reason it's called *premium*. I don't care if it's a hundred degrees or thirty below – premium grass is supposed to be green. I *want* premium grass. That's what I paid for and that's what I want," he asserted.

"And I'm telling you...that's what you got, Ramsey."

A muscle in his jaw twitched. "Re-sod the complex, or you will never get another job from St. Claire Architects."

"Whoa, Ramsey. Wait a minute. I—"

"Additionally, I will open a full investigation on the project, track down the manufacturer of where this so-called *premium* grass came from and if it comes back that it's not premium grass, and I'm sure it will, I'm opening a fraud complaint with the BBB."

"Ramsey, there's no need for all that. We've worked together for years. You know me, man."

"Then you should know me—how I operate and what I expect from my contractors. I know every job won't be perfect but I want my workers and contractors to work as if they are striving for perfection. *This* job didn't make the cut, so how can I trust you with anything else? I can't. I won't, not until you show good faith and remedy this situation. The way I see it is, how this plays out is in your hands."

Craig sighed exhaustingly heavy. Losing a major client like St. Claire Architects would hurt his business. He knew it, and he knew Ramsey knew it, too. "All right, fine. When can I get my guys back out there?"

"You tell me."

"Next week, Monday. I can get a team out there on Monday. That'll give me time to order more sod."

"Good. I'll have my project manager meet you there promptly at eight. If your guys arrive one minute late, the deal is off. I will hire another company to do the job and you will never get another job from my firm."

"I got it, Ramsey. I'll take care of it."

"Good." Ramsey hung up the phone, frustration encircling him. He internalized the anger – even though he was alone and could punch a hole in the wall if he wanted – but he kept his anger bottled up, waiting until the fizz died down. Only then could he open that bottle and be himself again. He wasn't quite there yet when he heard Judy's voice come over the intercom to say, "Mr. St. Claire, downstairs reception just informed me that your wife is on the way up."

A smile came to his face. All the frustration he was experiencing immediately melted away at the thought of Gianna being in the building.

"Oh, and Sir, you have a meeting at 11:30 with—"

"Reschedule it. Nothing comes before my

wife."

"You got it, Sir."

Ramsey stood up, anticipating Gianna's arrival. Judy opened the door for her and when she did, Ramsey saw that Gianna was carrying a half-dozen cupcakes in a little box. She looked beautiful. Her hair was brushed down, dancing around her shoulders. She had on a black dress that hung down to her ankles and a pair of black and gold sandals. At certain angles, you couldn't tell she was pregnant. Whatever the case, she was stunning.

"Hey, you," Ramsey said, taking deliberate steps toward her. "What's this?"

"Well, since you made me feel bad for baking those cupcakes for Royal, I figure I'd let you be the first to try my newest creation."

Ramsey set the box on his desk, then returned his attention to her. "First of all, my love, I was teasing you last night."

"I know, I know," Gianna sang. "I still want you to try these, though."

"Really, because I'd much rather have these," he said brushing his thumb across her lips as if they were strings on a guitar. Tilting her chin upward, he lowered his mouth to hers, delivering a kiss that left her moaning. Weak in the knees. Mind, gone. Completely at his mercy. Her hands tightened around his biceps while he played with her tongue like it was his favorite sport. Her pulse pulsated. Baby did cartwheels.

When they parted, she looked into his eyes like she was spellbound just by being in his presence. In many ways, she was. She had the utmost admiration for him – had never met another man of his integrity. He was something foreign – a man she never dreamed of having because back then her dreams weren't infinite – only empty hopes that she was sure would never come to fruition, hence the classification of 'empty'. Now, she had him – the man of all men – and she was carrying his child. He was a blessing, but being the mother to such an extraordinary man's baby went beyond her wildest imagination.

"You were sleeping when I left this morning."

"I was. It was that massage you gave me last night...oh, was it good..."

He cracked a smile. "I'm glad you enjoyed it." He gave her another kiss – a small one in the center of her forehead. "I didn't get the chance to tell you I love you."

"I'm sure you whispered it to me."

"I did, but now I don't have to since you're here. In my office. I love you, Gianna St. Claire."

"Stop it. You're making me feel tingly all over."

"That's how I *want* you to feel." He took another kiss. "You have no idea how good you make me feel, baby. Before you came here I was so angry, I felt like I was drifting off into a black hole."

"Jeez?" she said, trying not to laugh but failing miserably. "Why? What happened?"

Running his fingers through her hair, he

said, "Something work related—contractors not living up to my expectations."

"Oh."

"And you know I have high expectations."

"Of course."

"And I wasn't pleased with some of their work. Then you showed up and just like that, my frustration subsided."

"I'm glad I could be of service, Mr. St. Claire."

Ramsey opened the box on his desk, removed one of the cupcakes and took a huge bite.

"Ramsey, I was supposed to tell you what kind they were before you dived in."

"Doesn't matter. I like everything you bake, and these are delicious. What is this you sprinkled on top? Pistachios?"

"Yes. I call them pistachio cupcakes. I ground a half cup of pistachios into the vanilla batter, then after I baked them, I used green tinted cream cheese frosting and sprinkled grated pistachios on top."

"Nice." He took another bite. "I particularly like the appeal these will have to the healthy eaters among us who will go after these cupcakes because they can justify the calories by saying they had pistachios for a snack."

Gianna smiled. "Right. It's the guilt-free cupcake, but not really..."

Ramsey finished off the cupcake. "What else have you been up to today? You look beautiful in that dress by the way."

"Thank you. I went to see Felicity. We talked

a little about the baby shower. She's getting with your mom later on this week."

"I meant to ask you...were you planning on inviting Geraldine to the baby shower?"

"I don't know. Should I?" she asked him.

"That's your call. Of course, I'm here for support. If you want her there, by all means, reach out to her."

"Okay. I think I may...not sure just yet."

Ramsey offered a single nod then ran his thumb along her jaw. "What do you have on tap for the rest of the day?"

"I'll probably go home, take a nap, then annoy Carson for a while."

Ramsey grinned.

"I think he's bored, Ramsey."

"Why? There's enough work around there to keep him busy."

"I know, but he's so efficient with everything, and everything has to be precise and perfect. If he burns something—well, not even burn...if he *scalds* something, he'll dump the whole thing out and start over again. And you should see how meticulous he is when he does laundry. He folds shirts like they do at those fancy department stores. And then if the floors aren't shiny, he will get on his hands and knees with a rag and a bucket and clean every inch of it. You're only that anal when you're bored and have nothing else to do. He needs some fun in his life. You should set him up or something."

"I doubt if the old man wants to be with someone. The loss of his wife broke his heart.

He doesn't talk about it, but he's still very much in grief."

Gianna nodded sadly. "You know what he's going through. Maybe you can help him."

Ramsey agreed with her, briefly reflecting on Leandra and the turmoil in his life after she passed. Had he not found Gianna, he'd be what Carson is now – lost and broken – hiding pain behind a heavy work schedule.

"Well, let me get out of your way," Gianna said glancing around his office. "I know you have plenty of work to do."

"I do, but not so much that I don't have time for one of those ten-minute kisses that may end up with us on my desk."

"Slow down, cowboy," she said, her hand flat against his chest. "That was before I was carrying our baby."

"It was, wasn't it? I suppose that's why you're carrying one now—can't keep my hands off of you. You're so good to me," he said kissing her lips. "So good."

Gianna lost herself when she kissed him, feeling his arms strong and possessively around her.

"Drive safe on the way home."

"I will."

"Call me when you get there," he told her.

"So, you want me *and* Carson to call?"

Ramsey smiled.

"Yeah, I know you have him checking up on me."

"But it's all for no other reason than the fact that I love you."

"I know. I love you, too."

Ramsey took another kiss – one that left him longing for more. "I'll see you around six. I'm going to try to get out of here early so I can spend some quality time with my girls."

A smile glowed on Gianna's face. "Okay. See you later."

# Chapter 19

Nearly two and a half weeks later, as Gianna approached the eighth-month mark of her pregnancy, the family assembled at Ramsey's Lake Norman home for the baby shower. Bernadette, Felicity and Gemma had set up the decorations on the deck near the pool. The family was there – the brothers – Regal, Romulus and Royal. Gemma was in attendance, of course, and Geraldine was there, too. Even Jerome showed up. And of course family friends of The St. Claire's came, including Bernadette's close friend, Harriet.

At first, the dynamic seemed off especially with both Geraldine and Jerome in attendance sitting at separate umbrella tables. Then, Siderra was intentionally avoiding Romulus, and it was odd and obvious to the people who knew them well. And then there was Regal...

Ramsey watched him eye-stalk Felicity's every move. The woman couldn't eat a grape without him watching her chew it.

They'd just wrapped up a baby-naming session. Bernadette had passed out paper and pencils, asked the guests to write down a name for the baby and place it in a pink bowl. Then, she handed the bowl of names to Gianna who would read the anonymous results aloud to get the family's reaction.

"Okay, here goes," Gianna said, taking the first piece of folded paper from the bowl. "The first name is Anastasia."

"Not in this lifetime," Bernadette said. "I will not have my grandbaby named after some cartoon character."

The family laughed together.

"Tell us how you really feel Ma," Regal joked.

"The next one is Rayne," Gianna said.

"Yes. That's my suggestion," Felicity spoke up to say. "Y'all remember that when Gianna chooses it."

"That's pretty," Geraldine said.

"Yeah," Siderra chimed in. "It's different."

Regal shook his head. "I should've known it was WB who came up with some bull like that. If mother didn't like *Anastasia*, what makes you think she'll like *Rain*? I can hear the kids teasing my niece now—'look, y'all. It's getting cloudy. Here comes the *rain*.'"

Ramsey chuckled along with Regal. Bernadette found herself tickled, too.

Felicity wasn't amused in the least. "It's spelled, R-A-Y-N-E, doofus. Not R-A-I-N."

"It doesn't matter how it's *spelled*. What matters is how it sounds."

"And you sound silly."

"Yeah, well I didn't suggest to name my niece *rain* so who's the silly one?" Regal challenged.

Felicity narrowed her eyes. "Whatever."

"Okay you two," Royal jumped in to say. "Gianna has more names to read. Continue Gianna."

Gianna pulled another name from the bowl and said, "Ooh, I like this one. Rianne...it has two 'Ns' like my name and begins with an 'R' like her daddy's name." She glanced up at Ramsey and watched him wink at her. A smile touched her lips. She pulled out another piece of paper, saw the name and giggled when she asked, "Okay, who suggested 'Cupcake'?

The family erupted in laughter, but no one confessed although judging by the sneaky look on Mason's face, she decided he was the culprit.

She continued reading the other names – Elizabeth, Charlotte, Sasha, Paisley, Lilac, Lavender and Rose. Who wanted her baby named after a flower?

Following the name game, they played a round of baby bingo and another game where they split off into teams of two and used tissue paper to see which team could make the best-looking diaper on an adult. Regal volunteered to be the 'baby' for his team and Siderra was the designated baby for her team. However, Team Regal pulled off the victory, especially when Regal took one of the fake milk bottle props used for decoration and pretended to suck milk out of it.

And now, they took time out to eat...

Carson had a break from cooking since Bernadette decided to go with a caterer who made everything from the cake to the shrimp cocktail trays.

Gianna glanced up at the blue sky, soaked it all in while a warm breeze bathed her face. "This is perfect," she said. She was standing with Bernadette, Gemma and Felicity near the grill. "You all did a wonderful job. I appreciate it."

"You're welcome, dear," Bernadette said.

"Yes, you deserve it," Felicity told her.

"You deserve it all," Gemma said, excited, "And so does my little cupcake niecey-pooh." She touched Gianna's stomach.

"Wait...are *you* the one who suggested I name her 'Cupcake'?" Gianna asked.

"No. I think it was Romulus," Gemma said. "He had a smirk on his face when you read the name aloud."

Gianna smiled. She would've never guessed Romulus would've done that since he didn't seem to have a sense of humor. He was always serious about everything. Very cut and dry. Matter of fact. Maybe he was loosening up a little. Gianna was going to say something to this effect when she grimaced just slightly as she rested her left hand on her stomach. Was that a contraction? She'd never felt anything similar to it before, but quickly plastered a smile on her face so as not to alert anyone. Soon after, there was another one. She rubbed her stomach and took a sip of water.


RAMSEY HAD JUST prepared a plate of shrimp cocktail and walked over to where Royal was standing. Royal had his eyes on the women because *his* woman was there, but he saw something that raised his concern. He looked at Ramsey and asked, "How far along is Gianna?"

"She's a few days shy of eight months. Why?" Ramsey tossed a shrimp into his mouth.

"It's probably nothing, but I've watched her grimace a few times and hold her stomach."

Ramsey looked over to where Gianna was standing. "Just now?

"Yeah, while she's over there talking to the women."

Ramsey set his plate on the nearest table and made a straight line for her. "Excuse me, ladies. I need to borrow my wife for a moment."

"What's wrong?" Gianna asked.

He took her by the hand and led her to a private area of the yard where they weren't in earshot of anyone asked, "Are you okay?"

"Yes," she said. "I just felt like I was having contractions for a moment there."

"Then we're going to the hospital."

"No, Ramsey. These aren't labor contractions. They're just the ones they told us about in the pregnancy class, remember? The fake ones?"

"How do you know they're fake?"

"Because it's just as the doctor described them. My stomach gets really tight, then it releases. It's a little uncomfortable, but it's bearable."

"Okay, but that doesn't bring me any relief,

baby."

"Ramsey, I don't want to leave the family here and run off to the hospital. I'm fine. I am. Just trust me."

Ramsey sighed heavily, remaining equally worried. "If they don't stop, we're going to the hospital as soon as this is over."

"Okay."

He took her in his arms. "When was the last time you felt them?"

"About five minutes ago."

"And not since?" he asked, placing his hands on her stomach.

"No."

"Okay. Are you enjoying yourself otherwise?"

"I am. I was just telling your mom how nice this is. And it's such a beautiful day. It's like the universe is accepting our daughter, welcoming her to a new life."

"That's a beautiful way of putting it," Ramsey said. He glanced at her lips, then back up to her eyes. "Oh, and by the way, Rianne was my suggestion."

"I figured that out when you winked at me."

"What do you think about it?"

"It has a nice ring to it. Rianne St. Claire. I like it."

"I thought you would." Ramsey took her by the hand again as they walk back toward the festivities. "I'm going to watch you like a hawk for the rest of the day, but if you think anything is wrong, you call out to me. Understood?"

Gianna smiled. "Yes, Ramsey. I will."

SOMEHOW, GERALDINE AND Jerome were busy talking about the old times when they were together.

Bernadette was telling Harriet how excited she was to become a grandmother.

Siderra was standing at the food table helping herself to chips and dip while checking her phone when Romulus walked up and stood beside her.

"Never known you to be so attached to your phone," he said.

She looked up at him, her breathtakingly fine best friend, realizing that lately, she'd been trying her best to avoid him. Why? Because she was falling in love with him, but she knew those feelings would never be reciprocated by Romulus because he wasn't the fall-in-love type of guy, and he especially wasn't interested in her. He went for the flashy, figure-eight type – not the artsy girl who made crafts for a living. The more she thought about it, the more she resented him. She knew it wasn't fair to him because he didn't have any idea why she'd been giving him the cold shoulder, but that's how she was feeling at the moment. She looked away from him when she responded, "Well, I do have a business to run."

He couldn't pinpoint the nature of her mood swing. Seemed she was getting along with everyone else, but now that *he* was talking to her, she had an attitude. "So, where is the phone when *I* try to call you these days?" he asked. "You rarely answer calls from me anymore and don't tell me it's all because of the *business*."

"It's just a new—no, not new—a different mindset."

"Yeah, and what's this *mindset's* name?"

She gave him a hard glare. "None of your business, Rom. I don't pry my way into your life and who you may or may not be seeing. Give me the same respect."

"I do *respect* you," he said firmly with an edge to his tone. "And whoever I'm with, I don't ignore your phone calls. How about you extend that same courtesy to me? And if you're not going to be at a family dinner, at least let me know so I'm not caught off guard."

She felt an instant headache. What he didn't know was, she hadn't planned on being at any more of *his* family dinners because while she loved his family, they weren't *her* family. In her mind, she'd held out hope that one day they would be, but as the years passed by, her hopes of actually being a *real* family member fell by the wayside. Romulus didn't like her in *that* way and she couldn't torture herself any longer – sitting at dinner pretending to be happy when all she wanted was to be his wife. She wasn't about to tell him this now and possibly ruin Gianna's baby shower, so she responded, "Duly noted," and ate another chip right before walking away from him.

He threw up his hands, confused.

FELICITY STEPPED AWAY from the women to

try the mini-tuna croissant. She put three on her plate. As soon as she took a bite, Regal walked up behind her and said, "Uh oh...here comes the *Rayne*." He chuckled. "I'ma start calling you Rayne."

She rolled her eyes, then held a napkin over her mouth when she asked, "Can't you find somebody else to pester?"

"Nope. I'm all yours," he said, taking one of the croissants from her plate. There was a tray full of them on the table, but he thought taking one from *her* plate would piss her off, so he did it and felt good about it.

"And what name did you come up with since you're so busy dissecting mine?"

"Charlotte," he said, trying the tuna.

"Oh, that's original..." she teased.

"Gianna never said she was looking for originality—just a name."

"Why Charlotte?"

"It's a pretty name," Regal said. "And Ramsey and Gianna met in Charlotte. Fell in love in Charlotte. Everything went down in Charlotte at that bakery. The name Charlotte has meaning. Meanwhile, Rayne, on the other hand, sounds depressing."

"That's your opinion."

"Nah," Regal said, taking a croissant from the tray this time. "I think everyone here felt the same way. Mom almost fainted when she heard Gianna say, *Rayne*. Rayne St. Claire...yeah, that's not going to work." He tossed back the croissant and obliterated it.

"Who gave you any authority?"

When he finished chewing, he said, "Oh, trust me when I say not only is Ramsey my brother, but I'm one of his closest advisers."

*Advisers.* Felicity rolled her eyes. "Well, ultimately, the decision will be made between Ramsey and Gianna the way it should be."

"Yeah, and you can keep *Rayne* and maybe name your daughter that. Rayne..." Regal smirked. Walking away from her shaking his head, he said, "Good one, Dub."

Felicity felt pressure build at her temples. She hated it that Regal knew how to press her buttons. It would be difficult avoiding him since his brother was married to her best friend and they would always run into each other at functions like this. There had to be something she could do.

"WELL, SON, YOU done did it now," Mason said, draping his arms over Ramsey's shoulder as they stood looking at Gianna.

"She's incredible, Dad."

"I know. I see the way you look at her and the way she looks at you. And now this baby is coming. You have a few gray hairs already, but when this little girl gets here...woo wee...then the real gray hair is going to spring through."

Ramsey grinned.

"You're going to guard that little girl with your life," Mason said.

"Just like I do with her mother."

Mason nodded. "Just remember you always have your family. I know nothing about raising a daughter but I did raise four boys into very capable men."

"That you did."

Mason patted Ramsey on the back. "All right...that's my pep talk for ya. I'm going to help your mother. I know she's looking for me."

"Thanks, Pops."

"Yep."

Ramsey walked over to Carson.

"Enjoying yourself, old man?"

"I am. It feels nice for someone else to do the cooking."

"I'm sure it does. Hey, has Gianna mentioned anything to you about contractions?"

"No, Sir. She's always holding her stomach, you know, in an endearing way—a motherly way, but contractions? No. If she were having them, she didn't mention anything to me about it."

"Okay. Keep a watchful eye on her this upcoming week. She said she was having the false contractions, but I need to be sure she's okay."

"Of course, Sir. I'm on it."

GERALDINE MADE HER way over to Gianna when she finally saw her standing alone. "Nice baby shower," she said.

"Thanks. Gemma, Felicity and my mother-in-law put it all together."

"Well, they did a good job."

"They did." Gianna bit into a white chocolate

strawberry as she glanced up at Geraldine. Not knowing what to say next, she said, "So, I saw you talking to Jerome."

"Yeah...we were just catching up, talking about how things used to be, you know."

No, she didn't know because from her understanding, Geraldine had left Jerome because he'd lost his job. What more was there to talk about? Jerome must have had a forgiving heart if he was willing to reminisce about the past.

After a few passing moments of awkward silence, Geraldine said, "You're going to be a better mother than I was, Gianna."

Gianna wondered why she was stating the obvious. A *flea* would be a better mother than Geraldine...

"But where I lacked as a mother, I hope to make up for as a grandmother. I know I don't deserve that title either, but in the hierarchy of kinship, she will be my granddaughter and—"

"And just like I'm giving you the chance to have a do-over now, I'll extend the same opportunity to you to be a grandmother, Geraldine."

"You don't think your husband will stop you?"

Gianna glanced up and captured Ramsey's radar vision. The way he was looking at her sent chills all over her body. It was like he could see right through her.

"Uh," she said, losing her thoughts but when she looked away from Ramsey, she found them again. "Ramsey wants what I want, so no, he won't stop me."

"Okay, well thanks for giving me a chance. I know I don't deserve one."

"Just use it wisely, Geraldine."

"I intend to."

# Chapter 20

Tuesday morning, Gianna came downstairs holding her stomach. She was preparing to head to the bakery, but while she was getting dressed, she felt a warm oozing sensation between her legs. She looked down, fearing she'd see blood, but it wasn't blood. It was clear fluid.

Her water had broken.

"Carson," she called out calmly, surprised that she was able to remain calm under the circumstances.

"Yes, madam. You called?"

"Yes," Gianna said, still standing on the bottom step. Still calm despite the burn of the first real contractions. "Carson, my water broke. I'm going into labor."

"No, no, no," Carson said, panicking.

"Yes, yes, yes, Carson. The baby is coming. I need you to call Ramsey," she told him since she couldn't get to her phone.

Carson looked dazed like he didn't know what to do.

"Carson, snap out of it! The baby is coming."

"Okay," Carson said, dialing Ramsey's cell. "I'm calling him now." He handed her the phone and while Gianna waited for Ramsey to answer, she held on to the railing for support when a contraction hit. She bowed over in pain.

"Hey, what's up, Carson?" Ramsey answered.

"It's me, Ramsey."

"Gianna?" Ramsey said, already on alert, wondering why she was calling him from Carson's phone. "What's wrong, baby?"

"Um..." she breathed, trying to disguise the sharp contractions ripping through her body. "Are you at—at work already?"

"I just got here...walking into my office now. What's wrong, Gianna? Talk to me."

"I don't want you to panic."

"I started panicking the moment I heard your voice on Carson's phone, now talk to me, Gianna."

"My water broke."

"What!"

"My water broke, Ramsey. The baby is coming early."

"Okay, okay. Are you all right?"

"Yes, but these contractions are almost unbearable. I'm going to get Carson to take me to the hospital."

"Okay, baby," Ramsey said. "I'll be there as soon as I can. I love you."

"I love you too, Ramsey. Please hurry."

"I will, sweetheart. In the meantime, I need you to breathe just like they taught us in class, remember?"

"Yes."

"And stay as calm as you can for me."

"I'll do my best. Please hurry, Ramsey."

"I will, baby. Give Carson the phone."

Gianna handed him the phone.

"Carson?"

"Yes, Sir."

"Get her to the hospital as fast and safe as you can. We packed a hospital bag already. It's in the coat closet."

"Okay. I'll find it," Carson said. "Don't worry, Sir. The hospital is only a ten-minute drive. You know that. I'll have her there in no time. You, on the other hand, have to travel at least forty-five minutes to get here, so take your time. Don't drive like you're on the Autobahn. We need you to arrive in one piece."

"Yeah, got it," Ramsey said when really, everything the man said was going in one ear and out the other. He ended the call, loosened his necktie, came out of his suit jacket popped off his cufflinks and ran down ten flights of stairs since the elevator was too slow for how fast he wanted to move at the moment. He needed to get to the hospital. There's no way he'd miss the birth of his daughter.

He jumped in the Audi and hit the gas. Once he merged onto Interstate 77, he called his mother doing close to ninety miles per hour.

"Hey, Ramsey."

"Ma, get to the hospital. Gianna's in labor."

"In labor!"

"Yes, it's happening. I'm driving from Charlotte, too. I was at the office this morning when I got the call. Get there as soon as you can."

"Lake Norman, right?"

"Yes. Lake Norman General."

"Okay, son," she said, winded. "I'll be on the road soon."

Next, Ramsey dialed Royal. His brain was working so fast, he hadn't bothered telling his brothers what was going on before leaving the office. He just ran.

"What's up, boss?" Royal answered.

"I figured Gianna would have called Gemma by now but she's probably so scared and confused—"

"Ram, what's going on?"

"Gianna's in labor. I'm on my way to the hospital—Lake Norman General," he said, navigating through traffic. "Call Gemma."

"Okay...we'll be there asap."

Ramsey called Regal next.

Regal answered, "Ay, I saw you running out the building like it was on fire. What's up?"

"Gianna's in labor."

"What!" Regal yelled. He was in the break room getting coffee. Nearly dropped the cup.

"I'm on my way there now. Do me a favor and let Felicity know. I need to concentrate on this highway and I doubt if Gianna called Felicity if she didn't even call Gemma."

"No problem, Ram. Concentrate on the road. I'll call Felicity and hit the road."

"Thanks, Regal."

REGAL IMMEDIATELY LOOKED up the number to Wedded Bliss on his phone's Internet then asked to speak to Felicity directly, telling the receptionist it was an urgent matter regarding Gianna. He knew that would get Felicity on the line.

After a few moments, he heard her say, "Hello? This is Felicity James."

"Felicity, it's Regal."

"Are you kidding me? Do you think *everything* is a joke? Here I am freaking out thinking something is wrong with Gianna and it's only *you*."

"Something *is* wrong with Gianna. She's in labor. That's the reason for my call."

"She's not in labor. She has another month to—"

"Ramsey just called me and told me. Your friend is in labor."

"This better not be one of your jokes, Regal."

"I wouldn't joke about something like this now get your butt to Lake Norman General if you want to be there for your best friend."

"Okay. I'm on the way."

# Chapter 21

Ramsey pulled up at the hospital, jumped out of the car and didn't stop running until he reached Labor & Delivery. Nearly out of breath, he asked a group of nurses, "Gianna St. Claire...where is she?"

"Are you the husband?"

"I am. Yes. Where is she?"

"Right this way, Mr. St. Claire." The nurse began down a cold, long hallway while saying, "It seems her contractions have slowed down a bit. Happened right after she arrived. Her doctor is in route as we speak and should be here within the next few minutes."

"Okay. Good." Ramsey stepped into the room and saw Gianna lying on the hospital bed connected to an IV, a heart monitor and another monitor that kept track of the frequency of her contractions. He immediately attached himself to her side. Kissed her. Went into protective mode. "Gianna, I'm here, baby," he said. He watched her eyes open slowly. He kissed her again. She looked tired already. Skin clammy. She almost seemed out of it. And her blood pressure was low, Ramsey observed. In all of her check-ups, he'd never seen it high or low.

"How do you feel?" he asked.

"I feel sick."

"Sick like you may vomit?"

She nodded.

The nurse went to get a small pan, just in case it got to that point.

When the doctor finally arrived, Ramsey greeted her with a barrage of questions. Gianna's temperature was slightly elevated...she was sweaty...her blood pressure was low...she looked tired...weak. Gianna had told him she felt nauseated.

"This could just be the way her body is responding to pregnancy. I'm more concerned about the contractions starting out so strong then completely phasing out, so let's see what's going on here," she said, putting on a pair of blue latex gloves. "All right, Gianna, I'm going to check to see how far your cervix has dilated."

"Okay," Gianna said softly.

After a brief exam, she said, "You are about six centimeters which is odd because your contractions have stopped. Also, there is some blood—"

"Blood?" Ramsey asked frowning.

"Yes which suggests there could be some hemorrhaging going on, but let's not panic. We're going to make sure baby girl arrives safely. Right now, I'm going to give you some Pitocin which will trigger your body to start contractions again, but I must let you know—if the Pitocin doesn't work, we'll have to do a cesarean. Remember we talked about that at your last appointment?"

"Yes, but I don't want a cesarean unless it's absolutely necessary," Gianna told her.

"I understand, and it may not even come to that," the doctor explained. "I just want you to prepare yourself if it does."

"Yes. Thank you," Ramsey said. Still holding Gianna's hand, he said, "We'll be fine, Gianna. Everything will be okay."

"How do you know that?" she asked him.

Her question took him by surprise for a second, then he answered, "Because it *has* to be. This is a happy time for us."

"Easy for you to say. You're not about to push a whole, big person out of your body." She chuckled a bit.

So did he. "You can do it, Gianna." He wiped sweat from her forehead. "I have all the confidence in the world in you. You're strong and you've endured so much. You can do anything. You hear me?"

She was staring at him like she was in a daze. An eerie peaceful calm over her face.

"Gianna, do you hear me?"

She smiled just barely and whispered, "Love you," then everything went dark. Monitors went crazy with beeps and piercing alerts. She was out.

"Gianna!" Ramsey said, his heart racing so fast, he felt dizzy.

The room instantly filled with medical personnel – a bunch of attending nurses, Gianna's doctor and other doctors he didn't know. Ramsey held Gianna's hand tight, didn't want to let go even though two nurses tried to pry his hand away. He didn't want to let go. Letting go meant things he didn't want to think about.

The doctors quickly got her pulse back, but she wasn't doing good. Blood pressure still low. She was out of it and now the focus was on getting their daughter delivered. One of the nurses unlocked the wheels that kept the bed from moving. They had to move now – to the operating room. An emergency cesarean was the only option at this stage. Gianna couldn't push. She was too out of it to do anything. And she was bleeding abnormally. Shaking.

The doctor didn't have time to explain every detail to Ramsey and he realized this so he stayed out of the way, feeling helpless, trusting that the doctors would do their job – deliver his daughter and stabilize his wife.

Their baby girl's first cries brought tears to Ramsey's eyes. He'd gotten a glimpse of her before the nurses whisked her away to suction her nose and clean her up and then she cried more – sounded like a sweet melody to Ramsey's ears. She was perfect – six pounds, two ounces he heard one of the nurses say. After they got her measurements and footprints, they swaddled her, then handed her to Ramsey.

He smiled, looking down at his daughter – his creation – completely in awe and amazement but he couldn't rejoice like he wanted. Couldn't enjoy the smell of her. The cute little button nose and all the other features that were her mother's. His heart was heavy with worry. Gianna wasn't doing so well.

"What's going on?" Ramsey asked the doctor. "Is she okay?"

"We've managed to get the bleeding under control. We're giving her medication via the IV, but she's not out of the woods just yet. She's going to need time to heal and rest. She's still critical at this point."

"Critical?" Ramsey blinked back wetness, still holding his daughter close to his heart. Their daughter.

"Yes. We're taking her to the intensive care unit for recovery. I know you want to be with your wife, but unfortunately, the baby can't be up there in ICU. We'll have to take her to the nursery."

Ramsey grew conflicted. He couldn't be at two places at the same time and needed to be by Gianna's side. At the same time, he didn't want to let his daughter go to the nursery. He wanted to hold her. Love her. Admire her.

"Don't worry, Mr. St. Claire. Our team of nurses is the best in the state. Your daughter will be well taken care of and you can come by and see her anytime you like."

Ramsey didn't respond. He didn't know how. Didn't expect this. None of it. Everything was supposed to go smoothly. Gianna was supposed to have the baby, and they were going to be reunited in a recovery suite for a few days where all the family could come visit, see and hold the baby for the first time, then they would be released to go home. But Gianna was critical and now, baby girl had to go to the nursery alone.

"I'll take the baby to the nursery," one of the nurses said reaching for her.

Ramsey didn't move a muscle. He didn't want to let his daughter go just yet.

"Don't you want to go and give the family an update," she asked.

"No," he said. "I'm not leaving Gianna's side. Can you give my family an update for me please?"

"I sure will, Mr. St. Claire, after I take the baby to the nursery."

Ramsey didn't want to, but he handed baby girl to the nurse finally and walked up to ICU while the nurses wheeled Gianna's bed toward the elevator.

As promised, the nurse went to talk to the family and explained all that led up to Gianna receiving an emergency C-section. She told them the baby was okay, but Gianna was in intensive care.

Bernadette immediately burst into tears. Mason consoled her as best as he could.

Gemma couldn't control her emotions at the thought that Gianna – her sister, who in many ways felt like her mother – was in intensive care. Royal wrapped her in his arms – told her everything was going to be okay.

Felicity covered her mouth in shock while her eyes teared.

Regal sat down and hung his head, trying to make sense of it all. He felt sorry for his brother. Ramsey didn't need anything like this to happen especially after what happened to Leandra. He could only imagine the thoughts flying through Ramsey's mind.

Romulus stayed holding up the wall, not making eye contact with anyone or saying a word about what was going down. He just stood there with a stoic face, figuring he'd wait to get an update directly from Ramsey. No one would really gauge the seriousness of the situation until they heard the breakdown of what happened and Gianna's prognosis directly from him.

# Chapter 22

Gianna had been asleep for hours. While her blood pressure changed constantly, it still remained lower than what it should have been. She breathed oxygen through a tube. She hadn't adjusted her sleeping position once. She remained flat on her back.

"Hello," a nurse, a different one from the afternoon shift, came in and said.

"Hi," Ramsey told her.

"Feel free to go to the café and get something to eat—talk to your family—stretch."

"I don't want to leave her."

"We are fully staffed in ICU, Mr. St. Claire."

"I don't care. I don't want to leave her."

The nurse didn't give up. She said, "It'll do you some good to go stretch, swing by the nursery to visit your beautiful little baby girl and get something to eat. How can you be strong for Gianna if you're not taking care of yourself?"

The pushy nurse had a point. "You're right. Uh...when can she start having visitors?"

"When her blood pressure improves. For now, we can't have her rest being interrupted by people going in and out of the room. You know what I mean?"

Ramsey nodded then scrubbed his hands down his face, exhausted. He stood up, feeling defeated. Feeling like he'd let her down. Like this was his fault.

When the nurse exited the room, he took Gianna's hand into his and said, "I'll be back, sweetheart." He leaned down and left a kiss on her temple. "Love you."

Ramsey walked to the door but paused before turning the handle to look back at Gianna again, feeling conflicted. He didn't want to leave, but he knew the family needed to see him and find out what was going on. Who could better give them an update on that than him?

He walked into the waiting room where the family had assembled and caught Gemma's worried eyes first.

Gemma got up, ran the distance between them and closed her arms around him. She broke the embrace and asked, "Is she okay?" desperately searching for the answer to that question in his eyes before he said a word.

"She's in intensive care, peanut."

Gemma sniffled. "So, in other words, no."

Ramsey pulled in a breath, let it out smoothly – reminded him of the breathing techniques he and Gianna practiced in pregnancy class. Who would've thought he'd be the one in need of those breaths? "She's resting right now."

"What all happened?" Jerome asked, sounding broken with Geraldine standing next to him looking just as disturbed.

The family corralled around Ramsey and he gave a further update, saying, "Gianna passed out right before the doctor was going to give her medication to induce labor. Up until that point, she was talking to me...told me she didn't feel well and then she fainted. They rushed her to the operating room to do an emergency cesarean, and uh..." He felt his voice giving way to fear. To anxiety. To the possibility that she wasn't going to be okay, but he paused. Collected himself. He needed her to be okay and he knew if *he* lost it right now, the family would all lose it, too. "Baby girl is here. She's beautiful like her mother, and she's healthy, but Gianna..." His lips quivered. "Her blood pressure is low. She's sleeping. Been sleeping for hours."

Mason threw an arm around his son. "She's going to be okay, son."

Bernadette nodded, steadily crying. "She has to be," Bernadette said, her voice unstable and broken.

Ramsey clawed back his sadness to say, "You can see the baby. I'm just heading to the nursery to check on her now."

"Have you seen her, Ramsey?" Bernadette asked, following him down the hallway.

"I have." He smiled. "I was in the room when she was born. I've seen her, held her, kissed her—I didn't want them to take her to the nursery, but she's not allowed in the ICU, so—"

"Did Gianna get a chance to see her?" Gemma asked tearfully.

"No, not yet," Ramsey answered, and even

that fact broke his heart. He kept on walking until he reached the viewing window at the nursery. "Stand here. I'll go in and move her closer to the window."

Ramsey went inside the nursery while the family looked on. Then, he instructed one of the nurses to move the crib closer to the viewing window. The family had a good view of her now – the sweet, little angel swaddled in a blanket.

"Aw," Gemma said, wiping tears from her eyes. "She's beautiful."

Royal wrapped his arms around Gemma, consoling her.

"She looks just like Gianna," Felicity added.

"She does," Siderra agreed.

"She got her daddy's eyes, though," Mason said. "Look at those beautiful black eyes."

Bernadette placed a hand over her heart, speechless.

Geraldine pinched tears away from her eyes. The baby reminded her of when her girls were born – how happy she was but yet didn't follow through with caring for them.

"She's a doll," Regal said, awestruck. "Amazing."

"She is," Romulus added. "That's my lil' niece."

"And my lil' grandbaby," Jerome said.

"Since baby girl is healthy, we need to rally our support behind Ramsey as he takes care of Gianna," Felicity said. "Regal, can you and your brothers take Ramsey to the cafeteria to get something to eat? Otherwise, he won't go."

"Yeah, that's a good idea, Felicity," Regal said.

"The rest of us will stay in the waiting room in case the doctor comes back with any updates," Felicity said further.

THERE WEREN'T ANY updates – well except the one about Gianna's status remaining unchanged and no one considered that a true update because there was no progress being made. Ramsey was back in the room with her again looking up all kind of information on his phone – reading up on cases like hers. He couldn't understand how she was perfectly healthy during the pregnancy and now in intensive care. And during all of her checkups, all was well. Her blood pressure, normal. The doctor had informed them that Gianna's due date could have been off a few days, give or take, but an *entire* month?

He looked at her. She looked exhausted and sick – like sick to the point that she couldn't fake being well – not that she could fake anything at the moment. He eased onto the bed next to her.

Watched her.

This was not how the day was supposed to end. They were supposed to be elated, not worried. They were supposed to be rejoicing over their new addition to the family. As much as he wanted to, he couldn't rejoice – not until Gianna was out of the woods, but when would that be?

He kissed her on the cheek, then pressed his forehead to hers so he was connected to her some kind of way. He needed to feel her warmth. Needed this closeness. "We didn't get a chance to finalize a name for our baby yet," Ramsey said, even though he knew Gianna was sleeping. "She's beautiful, Gianna. Our little girl is beautiful. She looks like you, I mean, I can see both of our features, but she looks like you the most."

His forehead remained connected to hers. He closed his eyes. Absorbed her energy.

The beeps from the monitors were driving him insane. Thoughts that she wouldn't make it out of ICU battered his mind and ravaged his heart. After tragically losing Leandra, he never in a million years would've thought he'd go through those same feelings again – feelings of helplessness watching the person you love suffer. The agony of not knowing what the next second, minute or hour would bring. The man in him told him to be strong – told him she was going to walk out of here. But he still had doubts. He'd lost a woman he loved before. Was it about to happen again?

Ramsey swallowed the lump in his throat, willing himself to keep the strength that made him into the man that he was. The man he had to be for her right now. Even after he felt a tear roll down the length of his face, he fought hard to stay strong. Wiped it away. Endured the heavy weight of anxiety on his chest. "I need you, Gianna. I can't do this without you. Can't imagine having to raise our daughter without you. I can't. I—I can't be who I am without you. How am I supposed to go on without? I can't, baby." His body trembled. Tears remained at bay. "I know you have what it takes to pull through this. I know you do and I need you to get better. For me. I need you to get better for our daughter. For Gemma. But mostly for me. I know that's selfish of me, but I love you, and I need you. I know in my heart I won't make it without you, Gianna. You are truly the love of my life and I can't live without you being the other part of me. So, get well, sweetheart," he said wishing he could lie beside her. Hold her. He had to settle for her hand instead.

# Chapter 23

Two days later and there was no improvement in her condition. The doctors were beginning to discuss tube feeding. And then a nurse came in this morning and said something that nearly made Royal's blood pressure rise to new heights. She told him he could go ahead and take the baby home.

"I'm not leaving this hospital without my wife," he told her.

She knew he meant it. "I understand, Mr. St. Claire, but the baby is being discharged and I have no control over that. She's a healthy, vibrant little girl and she doesn't need to be here. Is there a family member she can go home with until you and your wife are home?"

Ramsey stroked his beard. His first thought was to ask his parents. If they weren't willing, he'd ask Gemma and Royal.

He glanced at his watch: 9:41 a.m. He was certain his parents were in the waiting room by now. He dialed his mother's cell phone from the room, explained that the baby had to go home and before he could ask, she'd already offered to take her.

"Thank you, Mother."

"How are you holding up, son?"

"I'm doing the best I can. I just wish she would give me a sign—something to let me know she'll be okay. It's been going on three days now and nothing. She's just lying here— the doctors are talking about tube feeding now."

"Oh, no—I'm so sorry, son. I wish there was something I could do."

"You're taking Rianne home. That's a lot."

"Rianne...that's her name?"

"It's not official, but Gianna liked that name, so for now, she's Rianne."

"Okay. Are you going to come down here and talk to everybody?"

"Everybody?" Ramsey asked.

"Yes. We're all here. Your brothers, your father, Gemma, Felicity, Siderra, Geraldine, Jerome and Carson. Harriet's here, too."

"Okay. I'll come down but only for a few minutes."

When Ramsey was off the phone with his mother, he took a much-needed deep breath, left a kiss on Gianna's temple and told her he loved her before leaving the room.

It warmed his heart to see his family all there on a Thursday morning to support him.

"Good morning, everybody," he said. "Um—" he blew a breath. "There hasn't been any changes with Gianna yet. She's definitely not leaving today, but the baby is going home with Mother. Please help her out as much as you can and spoil my little girl rotten until me and Gianna can do it."

"You have nothing to worry about on that

front. We got this," Regal said.

"I'm staying here," Gemma said. "I can't leave my sister."

"And I'm not leaving you, so I'm staying, too," Royal told her.

"That's fine," Ramsey said. "Romulus...Regal, I'm going to need you two to check in at the office to make sure all is well. You don't have to stay, but I at least need to know that there's order there."

"Will do," Romulus said.

"Um..." Ramsey dug around in his pocket for his keys. "Dad, there's a car seat in the back seat of my car. Can you get it and bring it in here? Baby girl has to leave the building in a car seat."

"Sure, son," Mason said, taking the keys.

"What can I do, Ramsey?" Felicity asked.

"Ah..." Ramsey threaded his hands behind his head. "Help out where you can with the baby. She'll need infant formula. I'll text you the brand name."

"Okay."

Ramsey took out his wallet and handed her two, one-hundred-dollar bills. "Pick up some diapers and some clothes."

"Will do. As a matter of fact, I'll leave with your parents, pick up all the items and meet back up and their home, if that's okay, Bernadette."

"That's fine with me," she answered.

"Good. I appreciate it, Felicity."

"No problem."

Mason came walking into the room with the

car seat. Ramsey notified the nurse that the car seat was ready and she brought the baby down, carefully lowered her into the car seat and buckled her in.

Ramsey looked at his baby girl adoringly, kissed her soft, little cheek and said, "I'll see you soon, baby girl." He looked up at the family and said pleadingly, "Take care of her."

"Don't worry, son. You know your mother won't let anything happen to this precious, little girl."

"She's adorable," Geraldine said. She looked at Bernadette and Mason when she asked, "Do you mind if I come over to the house to spend some time with her?"

"Not at all. I'm sure Gianna would like that," Bernadette said.

Ramsey nodded.

Bernadette gave her son a long, supportive hug. "We'll take good care of her and you take care of Gianna."

"I will."

"Yeah, use those magic vibes you possess over her and bring my girl home," Felicity said.

Ramsey smiled small. "I'll do my best."

"I love you, son," Bernadette said, throwing her purse straps on her shoulder.

"I love you too, Mother."

And with that, baby Rianne left the hospital, taking a quarter of Ramsey's heart with her.

# Chapter 24

The family scattered to handle their assignments. Romulus and Regal made sure it was business as usual at St. Claire Architects. Ramsey had already informed Judy about his family emergency and so she handled his emails and other business appropriately. Felicity shopped for the baby and dropped off clothes, diapers and formula with Bernadette.

Every day someone from the family came by to see baby Rianne. Romulus had purchased some baby rattles and more diapers. And he got a chance to hold her for the first time, thinking about how much holding his niece made him think about his future. He never wanted children, but Rianne made him reconsider.

Regal just so happened to show up today while Felicity was there. Coincidence? Probably not. Normally on Fridays, Felicity would be at the bakery, but since the bakery was closed, she went to visit Rianne before she would return to the hospital to check on Gianna. She was holding Rianne, pacing the floor while humming a lullaby – Hush Little Baby.

Regal smiled. "You look like you know what you're doing."

Felicity glanced over at him. "Are you talking to me?"

"Yeah, I'm talking to you. You've had practice, huh?"

"A little. I'm no expert. I used to babysit for some neighbor's kids as a teenager."

"Maybe one day, you'll be holding one of your own," Bernadette chimed in to say.

Felicity stopped humming. "If I could get one without the headache of a man to come along with it yes, I would love to have a baby."

Bernadette giggled. "You are something else, Felicity."

Regal didn't respond. Just watched her.

"She's such a beautiful little girl," Felicity said. "And she smells sooo good. Why do babies smell heavenly?"

"Because they're little angels," Bernadette said.

"She certainly is."

Regal walked over to Felicity after he returned from washing his hands in the kitchen and said, "Gimmie my niece, woman."

Felicity raised a brow.

"Regal, that's not how you talk to a lady," Bernadette said.

Regal smirked. "She's not a lady. She's a Dub."

"Oh my God, Bernadette, I'm going to choke your son," Felicity said, mildly amused.

Bernadette laughed.

"Those small hands can't do anything to me, girl," Regal said. "They're about the same size as Rianne's tiny, little hands. Bet you can give her a high-five right now and y'all's fingers would match up."

Felicity was tickled, but she forced herself not to laugh.

"Go 'head, Felicity. Give Rianne a high-five."

"You're silly. Get away from me."

"I'm waiting to hold my niece. Give her to me and then I'll get away from you."

*Ugh,* Felicity grunted. She wasn't done bonding just yet and Regal was nagging her. "Okay, Rianne. It's time to go to your crazy uncle. Please don't let him be a bad influence on your life," she said carefully transitioning the baby into Regal's large, muscly arms. "Make sure you support her head and don't hold her too tight with those bulky arms."

"I got this," he said.

"Oh, right. I'm sure this isn't your first time holding a baby seeing as how you probably have plenty of them littered around Charlotte and the surrounding suburbs."

Regal chuckled. "That's where you're wrong, baby hands. I don't have any children, yet. You interested?"

She grunted again. "On that note, I'm out. See you later, Bernadette."

Bernadette was laughing, but managed to say, "See you later, Felicity."

* * *

Gemma went up to the ICU to sit with Gianna since Royal had to make Ramsey take a break. While she was there, she looked at her sister, held her hand, felt more sadness come to her eyes.

"I'm supposed to be the sick one, not you," Gemma said. "You're the strong one. The fighter. The one who always got it figured out. So figure it out this time, Gianna. We're counting on you. Baby Rianne is counting on you. We need you. You know that, don't you?"

Gemma dabbed the corners of her eyes with some tissue. Sniffled. "I remember when I was young...in school...I used to get off the bus and run to the house. You were always there, waiting for me, preparing something for us to eat, helping me with my homework. At night, you would sing me to sleep with your silly, made-up songs—remember that?—and you woke me up in the mornings and did it all over again the next day. I appreciate you for everything you did for me." She sniffled. "I'm stronger because of you. Now, I'm asking you to channel that same strength to help yourself."

Gemma, still holding Gianna's hand, dropped her head.

"I—" Gianna said.

Gemma's head darted up when she heard her sister make a sound. "Gianna?"

"I remember...the songs," Gianna said faintly.

Gemma's eyes brightened. Hope came alive. Her sister was talking. "You do?"

"I do." Gianna smiled just barely, but she had yet to open her eyes.

"Gianna, we're all worried about you. How do you feel, sis?"

"I feel like I just had a baby, then got ran over by an eighteen-wheeler."

Gemma tried not to laugh as tears of happiness formed in her eyes. "Why are you talking with your eyes closed? Open them."

When she did, Gemma knew at that moment, her sister was going to be okay. "Oh my God, Gianna, you scared me," Gemma said, kissing Gianna's cheek, then all over her face.

"Get those *Royal* lips off of me," Gianna teased. Smiled softly. "Where's Ramsey? Where's my baby? Is she okay?"

"She is. Ramsey is in the cafeteria with Royal. I'll go get him for you, okay?"

"Okay."

RAMSEY COULDN'T STOMACH much. He nibbled on a few tomatoes and cucumber slices that he picked out of a salad. He was quiet, Royal noticed. He didn't want to discuss the situation anymore. Just wanted it to be over. Wanted Gianna and Rianne home. Wanted them to be a family.

"You know she's going to be okay, right?" Royal asked, glancing up at Ramsey.

Ramsey sipped water. Remained silent. Lost in his thoughts.

Royal hadn't seen him like this since Leandra. He was disheveled in appearance. Beard, unruly. Clothes looked as tired as he was. "Do you know how I know that? That Gianna's going to be okay?" Royal asked. "It's because she's strong, like her sister. Like

Gemma. And because she can take the heat. You know that saying, *if you can't stand the heat get out of the kitchen*? Well, Gianna can take the heat. Literally. She's in the kitchen all day long baking. Creating. Doing what she loves. She can take the heat." Royal chuckled a bit then said, "Look at everything she's overcome already. She raised her sister, kept the bakery open, she's trying to repair issues with her mother again, trying to make up for the years of not knowing her father and managed to marry the most stubborn, hardworking man I know."

Ramsey's lips quirked into a smile.

"Gianna isn't one of those women who fold, give up and wave a white flag. She's only resting, Ramsey. Healing her body. Preparing for the next phase of her life with you and the baby."

Still, Ramsey remained silent. Funny the things you remember about someone when you think you are on the verge of losing them. He recalled the first time they met...the dusting of flour on her nose...her smile...her uneasiness. He recalled how her voice sounded when she asked if he wanted a large coffee. She was nervous then and those nerves remained to this day but not as prevalent as they were before – like when they were on their first date and she spilled water all over the table and ran out of the restaurant. He thought about how her hand twitched whenever he held it. The way she chewed on her lip. Clammed up over the phone. Nearly freaked out when she woke up to find him in her bedroom that day. He remembered how she gasped, how her entire body quaked against his the first time they made love. He could hear her moans. Screams. Could feel her nails digging into his shoulders. He admired the way she took care of Gemma...how she put other people's needs ahead of her own because that's just who she was as a person. She had a heart of gold.

Royal was right. She'd never given up before. She may have *wanted* to, but she didn't. What would make him think she'd do it this time?

Ramsey glanced up at Royal and said, "You're right. You're absolutely right. Gianna's come too far to give up now."

"Just like Gemma."

Ramsey nodded, then drank more water. "I would feel a lot better if I had a sign...if her blood pressure will return to normal. I'd even consider seeing her eyes open as an improvement at this point. It's been days since I've seen her eyes. Those beautiful, brown eyes..." Ramsey dropped his head. Absorbed pain.

Royal looked up and saw Gemma walking toward them. She sat down.

"You've been crying," Royal noticed.

"Yeah, I have," she said, smiling.

"I thought you were going to stay with Gianna until I returned?" Ramsey asked her.

"That was the plan, but then she woke up and asked for you."

Without asking any further questions Ramsey immediately got up and ran for the stairs. He didn't stop running until he was standing next to Gianna. Her eyes were closed when he stepped into the room.

"Gianna?" He held and gripped her hand. "Gianna, do you hear me?"

Her eyes, the color of cinnamon opened up to him. She smiled, the kind of smile that told him she wasn't feeling all that well but it was enough to let him know she was okay.

"Oh, Gianna," he said lowering his face to touch hers. Forehead to forehead, he said with tears in his eyes, "You had me so worried, baby."

"I'm sorry," she said softly, barely audible.

"How are you feeling?"

She closed her eyes. Paced herself. She opened them again and said, "Gemma didn't tell you? I told her I feel like I've been run over by an eighteen-wheeler." She grinned.

Ramsey smiled and pinched tears from his eyes.

"Where is my baby girl?" Gianna asked. "Is she okay?"

"She's fine. She's a perfectly healthy little girl."

"Where is she? I want to hold her."

"You will, baby, but you have to get out of intensive care, first."

"I'm in intensive care?" she asked, surprised as her eyes scanned the room.

"Yes. You've been here for three days. You passed out and—" Ramsey sighed, not wanting to relive that nightmare. "It's a long story, Gianna. I'm just grateful you're talking to me right now because before I didn't know if—" he paused. "Let's just take this one step at a time, okay. Right now, I need to call a nurse to notify her that you're awake."

"Okay." Gianna yawned. "And can you tell her to bring me some water? My throat is a little dry."

"Sure, baby." Ramsey smiled, kissed her cheek again, then pressed the button on the bed to call the nurse.

# Chapter 25

Four days later, Gianna was discharged from the hospital.

She wasn't expecting a welcome home celebration but that's sort of what she received when she arrived home – a house full of family and food – a large spread of everything she liked, including buttermilk fried chicken – all prepared by Carson.

"Welcome home, sis," Gemma said. She and Royal had followed Ramsey and Gianna home, but she still felt the need to officially welcome her back.

"Yeah, welcome home, sis," Romulus said. "You, too, bruh," he said to Ramsey.

"Thanks, man."

Felicity and Siderra went to hug Gianna but Ramsey blocked them from doing so. "Hold up, ladies. I know you love her, but she's still recovering and very sore."

"Yeah, what he said," Gianna told them, holding on to Ramsey's arm.

"Do you think you'll be okay in the recliner, baby?" Ramsey asked her.

"Yes. That should be fine."

Ramsey helped her sit down and made sure she was as comfortable as possible. "Good?"

"Yes. Thank you, Ramsey."

"You're welcome, baby."

Gianna leaned back, reclined and breathed away stress. There was nothing like being at home, but what she wanted more than anything right now was to see her baby girl for the first time. Ramsey tried to show her a picture he'd taken, but she refused. She wanted to see her baby in person for the first time. Hold her. Love her.

Bernadette and Mason were still on the way with Rianne, but they were due to arrive at any moment.

"I'm glad you're back," Regal said, walking up to Gianna, touching her shoulder. "Now, you can keep Felicity away from me. She keeps following me."

"You wish," Felicity said.

Gianna giggled. "I see you two are still at it."

Felicity's eyes did a half circle as she walked away to get Gianna a plate of food.

"You gave us quite the scare, madam," Carson said as he came to sit next to Gianna.

"I'm sorry, Carson."

"No need to apologize. I'm just glad you're okay. The castle isn't the same without you."

Gianna smiled. "I'm glad you were there to take me to the hospital. Everything happened so fast. It was so chaotic. One minute I'm up and dressed, the next I'm having contractions." Gianna glanced up and caught Ramsey's gaze, then smile. "Did everyone get to see the baby?"

"Yes," Siderra said. "We were all at the hospital...saw her through a viewing room at the nursery. She looks like you, Gianna."

"Nah, I think she looks like her dad," Gemma said.

"She's a good blend of both of them," Romulus asserted.

Anticipation heightened, Gianna couldn't wait for Bernadette and Mason to arrive with her baby.

"They're here, sweetheart," Ramsey said after getting a text from his mom. He walked to the foyer and out the front door, then headed down to meet his parents in the driveway. When they parked, he opened the back door, anxious to see his baby girl. She was sleeping, but that didn't stop him from leaving a kiss on her soft cheek. "Welcome home, angel." He detached her car seat from the base then carried her to the house and up the porch stairs with his parents behind him.

He didn't stop until he reached Gianna, instructing her to stay reclined. He didn't want her to move and hurt herself. He unbuckled baby Rianne from the car seat then carefully lowered her into Gianna's arms. Tears bubbled in Gianna's eyes as she held her baby for the first time.

"She's beautiful Ramsey," she said as tears rolled down her face. She sniffled. "Oh my God. She's so pretty."

"She is."

Gianna slid her pinky finger into baby Rianne's hand. Her little fingers curved around Gianna's finger. "We made this beautiful little girl, Ramsey?"

"Yeah, y'all made her," Regal said. "We walked in on most of it...you know, when y'all were rolling around on the countertop and whatnot...supposed to have been making cupcakes..."

Ramsey chuckled. So did Romulus and Royal.

"Shut your trap, Regal, and let Gianna have her moment," Felicity said.

Hands up, Regal said, "I apologize little Rianne. Thank God your daddy didn't name you *Rayne*. With a 'Y'."

Felicity rolled her eyes.

Gianna, still cradling her daughter, gave a kiss on the forehead. Tears of happiness blurred her vision. She wiped them away. The pain she still felt from the C-section – evidence of it still hidden behind bandages – no longer hurt. She touched her baby's face – tracing her eyebrows. She touched her nose, her lips and said, "Hey, baby girl. I'm your mommy." She sniffled. Smiled. Her heart overflowed with joy. "She's so precious. Look at her Ramsey."

Ramsey smiled, admiring his girls.

"It's like falling in love all over again," Gianna said.

"Aw," Siderra said, bringing her hands together. "I can't wait to know what that's like."

Romulus looked at Siderra after she made the statement.

Ramsey glanced up at Romulus – more specifically at the frown on his face. He smirked.

His attention then went back to this moment

in his life – to his family all being here to support him and witness this touching moment of when *mother* first laid eyes on *daughter.* It was a delayed reunion but a reunion nonetheless and the only way he could describe it was sweet.

Sweet...

That's the word that would always come to his mind whenever he thought of his wife and daughter or whenever somebody asked *how's married life* or *how do you like being a father?* Gianna and their beautiful baby girl *was* his life. Gianna summed it up perfectly – it was like falling in love all over again and that was truly sweet.

# Epilogue

*One Month Later*

Ramsey left the office when he heard Rianne's soft cries from the nursery. Gianna was still sleeping, the reason he had moved Rianne from her bassinet in their bedroom to the crib in the nursery on the second floor. Gemma and Felicity had come over two weeks ago to help decorate the room using a cupcake theme as a guide. Ramsey especially liked Rianne's name in big, capital letters and pink polka dots on the wall by the crib. The curtains were sheer white with pictures of cupcakes on them. Her crib sheet was pink. Blankets pink. Even the walls were pink – same as Gianna's bakery.

He walked down the hallway to her room, scooped her light-as-a feather body up into his arms and asked, "What's wrong with daddy's baby girl? Are you hungry?"

She cried louder. He was getting good at recognizing what her cries meant. The high-pitched, screeching one meant she was hungry.

"You're ready to eat, aren't you?" he asked, holding her securely against his chest as they descended the stairs, heading to the kitchen. "Shh...it's okay, Rianne. Daddy's gon' make sure you eat."

Her cries eased up when they were in the kitchen. Carson already had a warm bottle ready and waiting on the kitchen table.

"You must've heard her crying, too," Ramsey said.

"I did, Sir...thought I'd make her a bottle for you. I know you need to get some work done."

"I do, but the family comes first."

"Of course."

"And Rianne doesn't play when it's time to eat."

Ramsey sat down at the kitchen dinette, cradled Rianne in his arms and gave her the bottle. That settled her.

"Looks like she has your appetite, Sir," Carson said.

Ramsey chuckled. "You think so?"

"Yes. Look at her go. That bottle doesn't stand a chance."

Ramsey looked down at his daughter and smiled. The little girl was a part of him. A part of his legacy. A miracle. She was precious in his eyes, just like her mother.

Carson flipped a pancake then took cooked pieces of bacon from another pan.

"She's going to be something else."

"Yes, she is."

"I'm glad to see Gianna up and about," Carson said. "Yesterday, she told me she felt like she could go back to work."

"She may *feel* like going back, but it ain't happening."

"I know I'm not going back yet," Gianna

said, standing at the kitchen's entrance with her arms crossed. She was watching him. She loved watching him with the baby. There he sat big and strong, handling tiny, little Rianne with such tenderness. Such love. He'd formed a bond with her. "I love seeing you hold her."

"I love seeing you, beautiful. Didn't hear you sneak up behind me," he said, looking at her. What a beauty...

She's just gotten out of bed, had on a white robe – the kind you find at fancy resorts – with her hair up in a messy ponytail. She walked over to him, kissed his lips then looked adoringly upon their daughter. She pulled out a chair, sat next to him.

"I'll take her," she said, reaching for her. Holding her, she rubbed her back gently to burp her then proceeded to let her drink more of the milk. "I can't believe it's been a month already."

"Me either, but I'm enjoying this time at home with you and Rianne."

"I'm enjoying it, too. Beth is doing a good job at the bakery while I'm off."

"She is. Maybe in a few weeks, we can take a drive over there just to see how everything is going."

"Yes, and we can take Rianne with us so she can see the place where her mom and dad met."

Ramsey smiled. "That would be nice."

"Yep," Gianna said looking down at the baby. She looked back up at Ramsey, holding his gaze. "It would be amazing." She leaned forward, kissed his lips, her moans filling the kitchen.

"See, this is precisely the reason I can't make pop-up visits," Regal said stepping into the kitchen. "Y'all up in here 'bout to start making cupcake number two."

Gianna laughed. "We were only kissing, Regal."

"That's how it all starts, ain't it?" Regal said. "I'm out. Ramsey, call me when you get your tongue back, bruh."

"Regal, wait," Gianna said, tickled. "Don't you want to see the baby?"

"I'll be back after y'all get done."

"Regal—"

Ramsey chuckled.

"Is he really leaving?" she asked Ramsey right before the front door closed.

"Yep. Sounds like he's gone. Now, where were we?" Ramsey asked, leaning forward, finishing what they'd started – an early morning kiss before breakfast.

# Reading Group Guide
RAMSEY (A St. Claire Novel)

- Describe Ramsey's love for Gianna.

- Should Gianna have consulted Ramsey before she met with Geraldine at the park?

- Do you think Geraldine is sincere? Why or why not?

- Does Ramsey overreact at dinner when he finds out Gianna met with Geraldine?

- Is Ramsey's issue about control or concern for Gianna's welfare?

- Do you think Ramsey is a good businessman?

- Does Geraldine deserve a second chance with her daughters? Is she sincere or does she have ulterior motives?

- Was Ramsey being too picky abut the grass issue?

- Regal says he needs love in his life. Do you think he's serious?

- What are your thoughts on the baby shower names?

- What do you think was going through Ramsey's mind when Gianna blacked out?

- How did you feel when Gianna laid eyes on her baby daughter for the first time?

**Thank you for reading, *Ramsey (A St. Claire Novel)*. I truly hope you've enjoyed it. If so, please take a moment to support me and my work by:**

-Writing a brief review on Amazon.
-Subscribing to my new releases email so you'll know what's coming next.
-Liking my Facebook page.
-And please visit my website: www.tinamartin.net

Thank you for your support!

Do you want to know how Ramsey St. Claire and Gianna Jacobsen initially met? If so, get The Boardwalk Bakery Series, consisting of the books: Baked With Love, Baked With Love 2 and Baked With Love 3.

Want to read Royal and Gemma's story? Get Royal (A St. Claire Novel) today!

Discover other books by Tina Martin:

**The St. Claire Series**
*All books in this series are standalone novels and are full, complete stories. Read them in any order.

Royal
Ramsey

**The Boardwalk Bakery Romance Series**
*This is a continuation series that must be read in order.

Baked With Love
Baked With Love 2
Baked With Love 3

**The Marriage Chronicles**
*This is a continuation series that must be read in order.

Life's A Beach
Falling Out
War Then Love

**The Blackstone Family Series**
*All books in this series are standalone novels and are full, complete stories. Read them in any order.

Evenings With Bryson
Leaving Barringer
Forever Us: Barringer and Calista Blackstone (A short story follow-up to *Leaving Barringer*. You must read *Leaving Barringer* before reading this short story)
The Things Everson Lost

## A Lennox in Love Series
*All books in this series are standalone novellas and are full, complete stories. Read them in any order.

Claiming You
Making You My Business
Wishing That I Was Yours
Caught in the Storm with a Lennox (A Short Story Prequel to Claiming You)
Before You Say I Do

## Mine By Default Mini-Series:
*This is a continuation series that must be read in order.

Been In Love With You, Book 1
When Hearts Cry, Book 2
You Belong To Me, Book 3
When I Call You Mine, Book 4
Who Do You Love?, Book 5
Forever Mine, Book 6

## The Champion Brothers Series:
*All books in this series are standalone novels and are full, complete stories. Read them in any order.

His Paradise Wife
When A Champion Wants You
The Best Thing He Never Knew He Needed
Wives And Champions
The Way Champions Love
His By Spring

## The Accidental Series:
*This is a continuation series that must be read in order.

Accidental Deception, Book 1
Accidental Heartbreak, Book 2
Accidental Lovers, Book 3
What Donovan Wants, Book 4

**Dying To Love Her Series:**
*This is a continuation series that must be read in order.

Dying To Love Her
Dying To Love Her 2
Dying To Love Her 3

**The Alexander Series:**
*Books 1-5 must be read in order. Book 6 and the spinoff book, Different Tastes, can be read in any order as a standalone.

The Millionaire's Arranged Marriage, Book 1
Watch Me Take Your Girl, Book 2
Her Premarital Ex, Book 3
The Object of His Obsession, Book 4
Dilvan's Redemption, Book 5
His Charity Challenge, Book 6 (Heshan Alexander and Charity Eason)
Different Tastes (An Alexander Spin-off novel. Tamera Alexander's Story)
As Long As We Got Love (An Alexander Family Novel)

**Non-Series Titles:**
*Individual standalone books that are not part of a series.
Secrets On Lake Drive
Can't Just Be His Friend
The Baby Daddy Interviews
Just Like New to the Next Man

Falling Again
Vacation Interrupted
The Crush
Wasn't Supposed To Love Her
What Wifey Wants
Man of Her Dreams

# ABOUT THE AUTHOR

***TINA MARTIN*** is the author of over 50 romance, romantic suspense and women's fiction titles and has been writing full-time since 2013. Readers praise Tina for her strong heroes, sweet heroines and beautifully crafted stories. When she's not writing, Tina enjoys watching movies, traveling, cooking and spending time with her family. She currently resides in Charlotte, North Carolina with her husband and two children.

You can reach Tina by email at **tinamartinbooks@gmail.com** or visit her website for more information at **www.tinamartin.net**.

67612335R00136

Made in the USA
Columbia, SC
29 July 2019